George H. Powell

Animal Episodes

and studies in sensation

George H. Powell

Animal Episodes
and studies in sensation

ISBN/EAN: 9783337230715

Printed in Europe, USA, Canada, Australia, Japan

Cover: Foto ©Andreas Hilbeck / pixelio.de

More available books at **www.hansebooks.com**

George H. Powell

Animal Episodes
and studies in sensation

ISBN/EAN: 9783337230715

Printed in Europe, USA, Canada, Australia, Japan

Cover: Foto ©Andreas Hilbeck / pixelio.de

More available books at **www.hansebooks.com**

Animal Episodes

and

Studies in Sensation

By

G. H. Powell

London
George Redway
1896

PREFACE

Of the stories collected in this volume three are reprinted from *Macmillan's Magazine*, two from *Temple Bar*, and one (at least, in part) from the *St. James's Gazette*, with the kind consent of the proprietors of those periodicals. A full account of the actual authorities for the more remarkable of the incidents described would, it is feared, occupy too much of the reader's time. It need merely be observed that most of the 'Episodes' originally came into existence in the form (here carefully preserved, as far as literary exigencies would allow), of narratives communicated to the writer by other persons, as to whom a few words of explanation and introduction have been added where this seemed advisable.

CONTENTS

IN PRAISE OF 'MOPS'

THE varieties of canine character have always seemed to me matter for the most interesting study.

What diverse degrees of morality, intelligence, and self-control separate, for example, that narrow and uncertain-tempered specialist the greyhound from the universally popular and trusty fox-terrier!

Not that specialists are all open to objection. One of the most lovable beasts I ever saw in the world was a lost foxhound puppy that I once met on the Surrey Downs. The grave pathos of his long face—humans have to make such 'long faces'—his anxiety to be recognised and taken home, and his gratitude meanwhile for a kind word, would have drawn tears from a stone.

But animals—human or other—that do only one thing, however well they do it, are subject to drawbacks. And reliable temper is of course the first question in a friend, four- or two-footed, that you mean to live with.

Such differences of character are not always indicated by expression. It is true that retrievers and other reliable animals usually carry about with them a conventional and somewhat fatuous smile, some eighteen inches in length—the smile which in the greyhound degenerates into something like hypocritical flattery, as in the wolf it becomes the symbol of hideous treachery. The demeanour of a fox-terrier is decently pleasant. But look at his cross-grained cousin—who could accuse *him* of looking artificially pleasant?

Strange—is it not?—that the ugly-muzzled, bow-legged little brute (with a liberal dash of bull in his composition), who has never been known to smile even when devouring a stolen mutton-chop, should lie so resignedly upon the hearthrug—where the baby never leaves him one moment's peace—although but an hour ago engaged in the perilous but exhilarating sport of pulling tail-feathers from a furiously indignant swan on the lake.

For this did his master—as the right man

may the right dog for the wrong action—hold the said animal at arm's length and ‘wallop’ it until weary of the painful duty.

A spectator might have noticed that the beast—which kills rats and cats with a grace and precision that amount to poetry—made several violent and successful efforts *not* to bite.

For that matter, as there are human so are there canine natures, and those not always the worst, that do not take ‘punishment’ kindly. The difference lies in a more refined sensibility both of soul and skin, and perhaps in a rarer, more feminine, if one may say so, and more spiritual nature.

Of such sort is the dog of whom we write. Mops is one of those long-haired terriers whom to know is to love. No one could ever venture to beat him; he would probably go wild with fright or passion; as it is, he has hardly ever had a rough word spoken to him, simply because in ordinary circumstances he is as good as gold. If his sensitive temper be ever hurt, that is generally the fault of some person who has approached him either without proper introduction, or in a manner unsuited to his dignity. It is his habit to mark these occasions by pretending not to know his dearest friends, as they pass while he lies on his particular mat in the hall; or (in very extreme cases) by retiring to the housekeeper's room, much to the elation of that elderly dignitary, and growling from the low and cushioned window-sill at all who venture into his presence with overtures of friendship. There are points in his character which, in such an animal, it is hopeless to attempt to alter; but these are not the low or mischievous tricks of common dogs. He would scorn to run after a chicken or a sheep.

Once, indeed, he caught a very little rabbit on the front lawn and brought it with tender fondlings, yet half alive, to bed with him in his basket by the drawing-room fire, whence the horrified housemaid removed its corpse during his absence at dinner-time. He has also been confronted with a live rat, with which, though exasperated by its want of humour, he for long endeavoured to play, till it bit him, when there was an abrupt end of the game, and of the rat.

But Mops has decided instinctive notions about how certain things ought to be done, and equally decided aversions to certain people. To Mr. Buller, the local banker, who comes over to dine regularly once a fortnight, he will never be more than severely civil. Mops' olfactory nerves have doubtless informed him of this gentleman's secret preference for fox-terriers, of which an adorable specimen is, at home, cherished in his bosom; but there possibly are other reasons.

Mops, it might be added, is as beautiful as the day, though this is not a very appropriate simile for one whose first appearance suggests a chaotic heap, or cloud of dusky hair, through which now and then you catch the sparkle of two gleaming dark-brown eyes.

> 'A dancing shape, an image gay
> To haunt, to startle, and waylay.'

At haunting, startling, and waylaying Mops is an admirable proficient; but it would be idle to say that every one regarded him as a phantom of delight. The old Rector, who is no sportsman, and, truth to tell, has intolerably fussy notions of the dignity of the human species, resents as undue familiarity what to the mind of Mops is a mere formal politeness. An eminent divine is, of course, nothing to him. Nor was there the slightest use in that dictatorial old gentleman screaming out to the butler as he entered the room — 'Now, keep that beast of a dog away from me!' Why, before the words were well out of his mouth, Mops, squeezing into the room in a frantic hurry, had rippled all over the sofa and its occupant, licked both the latter's cheeks with his long scarlet tongue, and was already out of the drawing-room window, and in full cry after a swallow on the lawn.

To more appreciative eyes it is a joy to see a being of such unbounded affection and enthusiasm, 'tearing' or rolling down the stairs to fly into the arms of some welcome arrival, or (supreme joy!) to be taken out for a walk by the right sort of person, usually of the male sex. At such a moment he will fling shrieking up and down the passage and over and under the furniture like an animated football; but when he stops dead short, or jumps upon your knees, shakes back his hair (which is really silver-grey, and, when combed out smooth, shines like the wave of a streamlet in the sun) —and, showing all his splendid teeth, grins ecstatically in your face, then indeed not the famed Peloton of Du Bellay,

> 'Faisant ne sçay quelle feste
> D'un gay branlement de teste,'

could be more bewitching. Having mentioned the subject of teeth, we must add that one of the greatest pleasures of Mops' life is to 'play at rats' with some competent human friend. This pastime (which is only allowed on the old leather settle in the smoking-room) consists chiefly in your trying to bury him in cushions, which should not be of expensive material. Then, if you have on an old velveteen coat, you may after a quarter of an hour come out of the game (which is deliriously exciting) with only a black and blue arm, for which you will be amply repaid by the sight of Mops erect, breathless, and in admired disorder, with his large eyes gleaming like coals of fire at you through their hairy curtain, simply dying to begin again.

He sleeps downstairs in the pantry—if indeed so sensitive and highly strung a being can be thought to sleep at all. The burglar would have a tread lighter than that of Camilla flying o'er the standing corn, who should pass within fifty yards of that 'rude heapy blackness' at the foot of the dimly lit backstairs, and not awaken Mops; and Mops once thoroughly awake and alarmed, it is a case of 'sleep no more' for other denizens of the same house, till he is pacified. Musicians tell us that if you only get upon *the right note* and *play it loud enough*, the vibration will bring down any fabric, as the trumpets of Israel did the walls of Jericho. This reflection recurred to me one night when a 'ridiculus mus' contrived both to catch itself and to upset the mousetrap in the kitchen about 2 A.M. At once the silver voice of Mops announcing this awful fact rent the silence of night into palpable and shuddering strips, and brought down the butler at the double, though fortunately nothing else. It is all right out of doors, in the open country. He is an early riser, and after a brisk turn in the garden, a brief and somewhat stereotyped *chasse* after the squirrel on the lawn, which he has long left off expecting to catch, he comes upstairs with the footman and the hot water. If he enters your room together with that functionary, it is then *de rigueur* to pretend to be asleep. There ensues a fearful scraping of the carpet—Mops taking off, he is not good at high jumps—a stumping and scratching up the bedside; a cheery greeting, and several histrionic bites directed at any exposed part; and further pretence is out of the question.

If he happened to be late, you may be awakened by a noise like a small and fine steam saw working spasmodically on the lobby just outside. That is Mops 'roaring like a sucking-dove.' It expresses a purely imaginary indignation.

It has been suggested that he is not what is vulgarly called a 'sporting dog,' and that is so. But though he has no idea of being all things to all men, like many an honest dog of our acquaintance, he can be anything he pleases (for his genius is rich and versatile) with the people he really loves. We often summon him to come partridge-shooting with us in the fields close round the house. If we find him not in the gun-room, we are used to give a low whistle. Instantly a responsive and piercing bark echoes through the back-premises,—Mops' demand addressed to domestics in general to open all doors that chance to be in his way. Then another, and louder, on the first landing, announces his approach. Then follows the noise of a carpet being dragged swiftly down the front stairs, — and there is Mops. But when one carelessly picks up a breechloader (which should always be done in his presence) as though it were merely a stick, his excitement boils over, and his yells are but gradually allayed as we get outside the front door.

Among the turnips and potatoes he presents the strangest figure, his long hair draggled with the wet, and his pointed nose and broad head (for once visible in their natural shape) peering up every now and again to see how things are getting on. Though a little slow among cover which often hides him altogether from sight, he will quarter his ground, work backwards and forwards at a wave of the hand, and set at his game in the most orthodox manner. · Mops, I verily believe, would scent a cockchafer; and the only fault in his pointing (a thing beautiful to behold in its amateurish energy and self-consciousness) is that it almost as often indicates the presence of a thrush as of a partridge. As to passing by any living thing two inches high, until it had been thoroughly explored by one or both of us, why, he would never dream of it. And when the day's sport is over, he will return, grinning like no other dog, his little legs plastered with mud and shrunk to half their size, and his splendid hair hanging down like a Cretan goat's, exhausted but supremely happy; and retire to the pantry to be brushed. For Mops is a robust animal. Indeed, a dog of this size need be strong to carry about pounds of soil and quarts of water in his coat all day. The coat, by the way, conceals the bull neck of his species, and the long and solid trunk is supported by substantial quarters and fine stout forearms, so that the animal is by no means only ornamental.

As to his use,—well, let this sketch be finished with the story of Mops' only real adventure.

Two years ago his owner was acting as land-agent in a much disturbed district of Ireland, and lived in a large and ugly mansion where, to tell the honest truth, some one else ought to have been living. But as an agent our friend, Major D., did his duty and was detested by the peasantry. At an earlier stage they had 'carded' one of his herds, drowned and strangled his calves, and even fired at one of his daughters (a pretty girl of sixteen) as she sat in loose array at her window one summer night. The bullet is in the window-frame to this day.

Her father, who was annoyed, replied with a shot-gun and two sawdust cartridges from a lower story, and it is believed, to some effect. This, however, is by the way. Once a week, at the time referred to, Major D. used to drive into the neighbouring market-town, and on these occasions Mops (considerably to his relief) had never shown the slightest wish to accompany him further than the park-gate. One Wednesday, however,—it was a day or two after some ill-looking fellows had been seen hanging about the park,—Mops suddenly changed his mind. He was determined to go. This was embarrassing for the Major, who, apart from the trouble of looking after the dog, was afraid of risking so valuable an animal in a locality so distinguished for what is called in Ireland 'agrarian feeling.' What was to be done?

Mops was carried upstairs the picture of

despairing misery, and locked into an empty room on the first floor, generally used for carpentering. His lamentable howls gradually subsided, and the rest of the household went about their business. Meanwhile Mops, as afterwards appeared, was doing a little carpentering on his own account. The door was a good sound door, but the floor beneath it was rather worn, which just enabled him to get to work.

It is a pity that no one could have seen his muscular little form as it lay there curled up on one side, the shaggy head savagely shaking as at each *scrunch* of his gnawing teeth fresh splinters of the deal board came away, and were swept aside by his little paws. It must have been hard work, harder than scraping at any rabbit-hole, but probably more delightful.

Nearly six hours had passed when an astonished domestic noticed and duly reported the alteration just executed by Mops. At that moment a small dark form might just have been discerned in the dusk of the evening scudding across the fields. This was Mops going to meet the Major,—and why, in Heaven's name, going at all?—and why going this way (the shortest cut as it happened) and not along the highroad? Who shall peer into the workings of that strange little mind, or whatever we please to call it?

It is certain that the point on the highroad aimed at by Mops, consciously or unconsciously, was just about where an intelligent being would have expected the Major to be if he were walking home (as a rule he drove) at his usual hour; and it is equally certain that the Major was there. It does not appear, moreover, that Mops had the slightest doubt of this, or indeed exhibited the slightest hesitation as to what he meant to do, throughout the whole course of this, his one really serious adventure. The Major was there, and nothing separated Mops from him but a high and rough stone wall, such stone walls as are peculiar to Ireland, where they have witnessed, and in their mute way assisted, many ugly deeds. One of these in fact was in process when Mops arrived, after a frantic struggle, on the top of that wall.

Only a few yards before reaching this point on the road, the Major, who for reasons of his own had sent the carriage on and was walking home easily and circumspectly with a cigar in his mouth and a double-barrelled shot-gun under his arm, was suddenly confronted by a ragged and dirty masked ruffian who seemed to have dropped from the skies, but who soon proved his infernal origin by firing a heavy horse-pistol of antediluvian date right into the Major's face. As the heavy slugs whistled by the Major's ear, the dirty ruffian turned and fled down the deserted road into the gathering darkness.

Our friend, whose temper had been soured by the society of a disturbed neighbourhood, leant against the wall for a moment to steady himself, and, allowing the conventional forty yards' grace, deliberately let off two barrels into and about the stern of his retreating enemy. The man howled fearfully, but continued his course. The Major smiled, but the next moment cursed his folly with a mighty oath, and turned to grapple with a second opponent who, having waited his opportunity, sprang upon him while encumbered with his useless gun, and in the surprise bore him almost to the ground. What this second monster, who was also masked and unshaven, intended to do with the rude agricultural instrument, a sort of broken sickle, which he produced at this moment, must be left to the imagination, for at this moment his attention was distracted.

With one of his curious little gurgling shrieks (like the bursting of a small musical instrument) the breathless Mops jumped, or fell rather, on all fours from the top of the wall. He did not spring at the man's calves, as dogs so often do; he had no time to think of that,—and in fact alighted a little higher up. The man wore moleskins, but what are moleskins to a little dog who makes a light afternoon meal of a bedroom door? Before any one of the three knew very clearly what had happened, Mops had buried ten little teeth, each sharp as a new carving chisel, in the most fleshy part of the objectionable man.

That was all, and that was quite enough.

The Major, who has assisted (in the French sense) at many an Irish row, and seen a good deal of service in Egypt, confesses that he never heard a man swear as that ruffian did just before he was knocked down by the butt of the empty gun.

That night there was a good deal of coming and going of police. One of the individuals arrested will carry to the end of his life (which may be conterminous with the end of his imprisonment) such a 'pretty pattern of No. 5' that the Major has more than once expressed a wish 'to send it to the makers,' which of course is out of the question. The other will remember Mops, I daresay, as well as any of us, but for a different reason.

MACHINA EX—CŒLO?

A METROPOLITAN EPISODE

THERE was a big fire—to speak correctly, two big fires—in London on the night when 'Emergency' Walford went to see his beloved. Walford's baptismal name was Henry, and the *sobriquet* here recalled was one which a few college friends had once suggested in memory of what had once struck their thoughtless minds as a salient phrase in his conversation. Among flimsy and meaningless epithets none perhaps stick closer than an ironically 'practical' nickname to a frivolously expansive and therefore presumably *un*practical individual, whose precious 'ideas' as to what he or his friends 'could' or 'should' do in any given improbable crisis of affairs are apt to appear a trifle too ingenious for an imperfect world.

It was beyond question, however, that Henry Walford and a party or parties unknown had once been inadvertently locked into the billiard-room of a strange and vast country-house by a somnolent butler, who long before their discovery of the feat had retired to a bourne beyond the reach of pantry bells, or indeed of any noise not calculated to waken a household long since lapt in the arms of Morpheus. Under such circumstances, embarrassing at 1-45 A.M., to open various clanking shutters, get out into the garden, and throw stones at what may or may not be the bedroom windows of highly nervous ladies or irritable elderly gentlemen, with whom you have but a superficial visiting acquaintance, seems to the boldest and the sleepiest an inartistic resource. Yet it would probably have been adopted in this case but for Walford, whose absurd fecundity of invention had of course been challenged in the bitterest irony to reveal another and better way of escape.

Yet in less than half an hour this imaginative individual, with no experience of practical burglary, had examined the heavy mahogany door, thrust under it (after pushing back the outside mat with a large paper-knife) a stiff sheet of paper, selected from the mantelpiece two of the metal instruments known as 'pipe-cleaners,' twisted them into a sort of pincers, and then with indefatigable labour and the assistance of a friend holding the candle at exactly the right level and pouring much wax upon the floor, twisted round the key, and thrust it out of the lock. Thence it fell inevitably upon the paper, and finally, amid a burst of muffled but enthusiastic applause, was drawn under the door, and the two, heated but triumphant, made their way to bed. Talking of keys, also, a friend, from whom Walford was once parting at some lonely village in the Tyrol, lamented to him that he had got to rise early next morning and had lost his watch-key. 'A confounded bore,' he added; 'my watch has stopped. Could you——'

'Pooh!' said Emergency Walford, 'wind it up with the key of your Gladstone bag. Hold it sideways.'

The reader is perhaps sceptical of this feat. If so, let him in some half-hour of leisure open the inner case of his watch, and try it. If the winding-up of a watch were oftener a matter of life and death, the experiment would be more popular.

It may be added that Henry Walford in his expansive moments claimed, with what degree of truth cannot now be determined, to have been the 'true and first inventor' of a number of useful and labour-saving devices, the lucrative evolution of which by other hands aroused in him no cynical jealousy whatever. The houses which he built—for he was himself an architect in small practice—fortunately exhibited no signs of abnormal ingenuity; and the prattle of one long-forgotten evening at college was presumably the remotest of all matters from his well-occupied mind, as he sauntered across spacious highways towards the little street in Westminster where dwelt, with her widowed mother, the lady of his love.

As he stood upon a pillared island in the thoroughfare opposite the oldest church in the metropolis, his ear caught the harsh and jarring cry—partly of excitement, partly of warning—which usually heralds the approach of a fire-engine. The phenomenon is not an unfamiliar one to the *habitué* of London streets; but Walford had for many years, in after-office hours, cherished a passion for dramatic adventure by practising among the few privileged amateurs attached to the Fire Brigade. He was, therefore, not much surprised to recognise the engine-men and horses of his own company, and shot an inquiry at the mail-clad Jehu as the latter pulled his pair into a hand-canter to avoid colliding with an unwieldy van. 'Amberwell Wharf ware'ouses; well 'light,' retorted a sailor with half-turned head, holding on to the rail behind. 'Yah-h-h!' said the foot-passengers from the pavement to left and right; and to the accompaniment of a *sempre diminuendo* roar, the smoking, clanging, glittering chariot tore away to the eastward.

On another occasion Walford would very likely have pursued or hailed a cab, and pelted —uniform or no uniform—to the scene of action; as it was, he merely gazed wistfully after the disappearing vehicle with a 'no-more-of-that-for-me' sort of look, and held on his course.

The course of true love had run quite smooth for Henry Walford; not that he and his *fiancée* were meeting to-night merely for the idle pleasure of the thing. There was a business in hand most serious to the female, and not indifferent to the masculine, mind—no less, in short, than the adaptation of the furniture of his own roomy bachelor 'diggings' to the more cramped apartments of their new 'bijou' family residence in a distant square in Bayswater.

Meeting, as it were, by appointment at the door of the little ivy-covered house in Old College Street, Walford and his *fiancée* were soon on their way to the very different yet not very remote 'neighbourhood' of Gloria Road, a large thoroughfare leading directly away into the heart of the wild and unfashionable south-west. As you follow it, walking away from the clock-tower, the fifth or sixth turn to the left brings you to the front of a large but not very prosperous-looking edifice hight St. Michael's Mansions, Catchbrook Street, on the seventh floor of which were situate the chambers above mentioned. This cheap and airy altitude Walford naturally spoke of as St. Michael's Mount. Indeed, on foggy nights the pile, if approached in a diagonal direction, presented, with the assistance of a 'shoulder' supplied by the adjoining factory and warehouse, a distinct resemblance to a well-known peak in the Bernese Oberland.

'Suppose we walk up,' said Walford, 'for a change. The lift's so stuffy and slow.' And the lift official had the habit peculiar to his kind of turning round and staring fixedly at the occupants. 'Don't hurry. Hook on to me.'

As a matter of fact, when they reached the door she tripped up lightly before him, and he ran after her, and so they both reached the third floor in a condition so breathless as to be incapable of intelligent conversation.

She was a sprightly, active little woman, with jet-black hair, now a little dishevelled, and dark eyes, eyes solemnly impressive till she laughed —they were both laughing now, as she finally condescended to take his arm—and then disturbing in quite another way to your very vitals.

That being so, there should, strictly speaking, have been a chaperon (who, however, could not have been expected to run up six flights of stairs), for in the whole house there were probably not more than two other people—a caretaker and his wife—somewhere downstairs, all the other occupied floors being offices, which were naturally deserted at such an hour. Not that any chaperon could have shown more anxiety for her safety when they had reached the happy top.

'It's a wonderful height up, isn't it? But I wouldn't lean out of that window.'

It appeared, however, that he would upon certain simple conditions, and with his arm encircling her small person in the most natural manner imaginable. He drew it closer, indeed, as at that very moment another murmur swelled up from the under-world. Again that ringing, metallic vibration mingled with the rapid beat of horses' feet, and, craning out of the window, they both caught sight of a second fire-engine threading its way—the driver half-erect over his dancing steeds—along the channel so deep below them, while straggling pedestrians scattered this way or that. Scarcely had he drawn his precious visitor inside again, when there was a louder roar, this time quite a cheer of triumph, as a third driver entered on the scene by a side street from the north, and, seeing the roadway clear, spread his team into a racing gallop over a straight bit of easy going. Walford leant out again just in time to catch the gleam of flying brass and a faint trail of vapour floating upon the evening air.

'They 'll be having a night of it,' he said half-sadly.

Indeed, long before the next sun rose a similar reflection was borne in upon the minds of almost every individual directly employed in the extinction of fires in the metropolis, from the 'chief' himself, whirled away from a fashionable dinner, in the middle of his favourite Indian anecdote, by the scarlet dogcart of inexorable duty, to the humblest salvage man that with savage glee ever fleshed an axe on costly mahogany furniture.

The efficiency of that important body, the 'Fire Brigade,' had, so said pessimist critics, been impaired by the injudicious changes of a newly constituted local authority. On the other hand, every one seemed to be agreed that there were grave reasons for increasing the number of stations, and that whenever a given number of fires, of a magnitude illustrated by recent examples, should happen to occur upon one and the same night, the date of the coincidence would very possibly be as memorable as the year 1666. Of course such an event was improbable ; but its abstract improbability became of little interest at a moment when three distant conflagrations were each occupying thirty or forty engines apiece, and the last pair of horses in the stables of the central office had to be taken from the coal-van to draw the one remaining steamer in the direction of a fourth block of buildings just reported by telephone as 'well alight.'

Walford's remark, however, indicated rather sympathetic excitement than anxiety, for which there was so far no particular reason, even had there been nothing particular to distract his attention.

'How dreadful!' murmured the Distraction, who was reclining at length in the best lounge-chair after the exertion of so unusual an ascent. 'I say, Hal, what capital arms you—I mean your chairs—have!'

'The better to—' (his quotation, which caused her to blush, was cut short by a severe fit of coughing)—'Ahem! By the way, Nellie, when you're rested, let's go up, and I'll show you the roof.'

Inside Walford's small 'flat,' which shut its own front door upon the public stair and lift-well, there was a private trap-door, accessible by a short ladder, leading on to the level plateau above. Around it ran a shuddersomely low balustrade of masonry, which he would hardly allow her to touch, all the more that he remembered once tempting the Providence lovers are so anxious to conciliate, by dancing on the top of it with a few thoughtless friends after dinner. It made him ill to think of such a thing now.

They sat down—she close at his side, and not unimpressed by the eerie height—upon some lead-covered erection in the middle. To the east stretched an oblong promontory, the other wing of the 'Mansions,' separated from the 'Mount' on which they sat by the deep gulf of a passage some twenty feet wide.

On all other sides London stretched away beneath them, north, south, and west, a level dusky forest of gable and chimney, dotted here and there with church spires like giant trees, and cut into innumerable deep 'rides'—regular fissures up which the thousand illuminations of street and shop were just beginning to throw their mysterious glow.

But under existing circumstances it was only possible to look in one direction—where over the wharves of Amberwell brooded and blossomed a crimson and golden rose of flame, blood-red at the heart low down, where it showed against a jagged outline of black, and purpling the long banks of cloud overhead.

Machina Ex—Cœlo?

For five, perhaps ten, minutes they sat and watched the finest spectacle that any great city can afford, and then descended to the sitting-room for the transaction of the business in hand. To this they betook themselves, when he had lighted the lamp, with a delightful air of seriousness, sitting each on one side of the substantial table in the middle of the room, she with a pencil in hand and piece of paper before her, he drumming on the table in pensive abstraction. The occupation had little of the romantic in it, yet the moments flew quickly.

'That small knee-hole table would go nicely into the bay-window of the drawing-room,' said he.

By rights they should both have been looking at the knee-hole table, and thinking of the bay-window. As it was, each caught the other looking at him—and her—respectively, in an absurdly surreptitious manner. This had happened before, and was followed by a resolution on the part of both to fix their whole minds upon the furniture question; and again the moments flew.

Several items had in fact been satisfactorily disposed of—partly through his having shifted his position to one nearer but not opposite to her—when Walford started up with a wild howl and ran to the window.

'Oh, Hal,' she cried, frightened and startled by his vehemence, 'what is it?'

'Paper,' he said, recovering himself with a quite unsympathetic promptitude. 'Paper and perhaps chemicals.'

Some three and a half miles away, from one of the heights of north London a stream of flame shot fiercely up into the night, and swayed and blazed, a pillar of fire that seemed to connect earth and sky; and again for five minutes they sat and gazed.

Fires, to the student of London at night, assume rich diversities of character. Some blaze with a condensed fury, suggesting that the dome of St. Paul's, inverted and filled with water, would boil over in three minutes on such a furnace. Others have more the nature of a showy pyrotechnic display, which, if it seriously alarms a few hundred people, rouses the dazed admiration of thousands of bored and *blasé* citizens.

'How awful!' she said; 'but it doesn't look so bad as the other.'

'But it is,' said he; 'they'll want more engines.'

'Why?'

'Because there's no pressure up there—not enough to wash the ground-floor windows with.'

'Pressure!' she answered innocently. 'I thought it was the engines always pumped the water up.'

The amateur fireman smiled sweetly. 'So they do,' he explained, 'when they've got to, but not when the water will go up of itself. Don't you see, Nellie girl, it all depends on the fall. You send a manual or steamer to most fires, because they are usually wanted, and to take the men, fixings, hose, etc.; but if the standpipes from the street were enough—— By Jove! It's lucky there's no wind; doesn't it flare up straight!'

'But, Hal,' she persisted, with the air of a studious learner, 'would a standpipe send water up here if we wanted it?'

He looked down to the street, which seemed almost deserted but for a newsboy running and yelling out some announcement which he could guess but not hear from the heights of

St. Michael's Mount. A few foot-passengers were hurrying along, obviously to get a better view of the great show; even the policeman had gone to the extreme end of his beat to satisfy a similar curiosity.

'No,' he mused meditatively, 'not up here, but anywhere near the river-level, you know, the hydrants will throw sixty gallons a minute over the tops of any of the houses. But of course, if your fire's had a quiet start by itself, you want to throw five or six streams further than that; why,'—he concluded, sitting down in the chair he had first occupied, and playing on the table—'you must have engines, and you must have 'em smart, and if they happen to be wanted elsewhere it's sometimes rather awkward. That thing up there,' he pointed to the window, 'would of course be seen directly all over the place. But then the Amberwell fire won't be got under to-night, I daresay—and when they get there, very likely there won't be water enough to fill a dam!'

'To fill a dam, Hal!' interrupted the young lady; 'what's that?'

'Oh, nothing wrong. Only a great sort of canvas tank—haven't you ever seen it?—that they put over the main plug in the street, and all the engines suck out of it—it runs over all the time, you know, if there's a decent supply; and they call it the "universal dam" (sounds rum, doesn't it? like something to do with the end of the world), because of course each engine has——Ah! there's another,' he broke off, as a faint rattle crossed the end of the street, 'and going north.'

These simple explanations, given from the height of quasi-professional knowledge, seemed to possess vast interest for their solitary auditor. It took the form of a purely academic ebullition of public spirit.

'Ought you to go and help?'

The lecturer turned away to hide a modest smile.

'Very likely they may be short of hands,' he answered; 'but I expect they'll do without me. Let's get on with the furniture.'

But after a minute or two of business, her mind reverted to the subject.

'Hal,' she said, looking up suddenly with a subdued and quite respectful chuckle, 'I wish you'd put on your fireman's things—you've got them here, haven't you? And I should so like to see how you look in them.'

And he, liking to see that mischievous sparkle in the black eyes, and not unwilling to give her some remembrance of himself in a character in which he did not expect to appear again, retired and donned the familiar uniform —at least the jacket, belt, axe, and helm of glittering brass, wearing which he reappeared in the doorway at ''tention.'

'Now, if you only had a spear,' she said, laughing with delight at his heroic appearance, 'you 'd look just like Achilles or some person out of "Lays of Ancient Rome"'; and she insisted on handling the helmet to see if it was real gold.

'It is,' he said, 'but hadn't ought to be. Should be black. There you stumble on a breach of the new regulations concerning volunteers, which however won't concern *me* much longer.'

'The garment,' he remarked, rubbing his buttons, 'apologises for not being Tyrian purple, which it should be, to suit Mamilius— wasn't that the Johnny whose headpiece "shone like flame"?—and as to spears,' he said, resuming his seat and scratching out a perfectly nonsensical entry upon a piece of paper, 'I can tell you a hose is as heavy and as difficult to hold straight as any "longshadowing lance." By the way, how about this table we're sitting at? would it do for the state dining-room? One thing, no slavey—parlour-maid, I mean—with more than an astral body would ever get round it with the flap out.'

'Oh, the table's simple enough,' she replied with necessary firmness; 'but I wish, Hal, you'd give your mind to that settee, and measure it now,' she added, getting up from her chair. 'If we could get it into the other window, you see, it would just hold two.'

'It does that already,' he said—and lo! they were sitting side by side again.

There was another momentary delay, whereupon, after what seemed a severe struggle, she took the foot-rule from him, and proceeded to measure, he obediently taking notes at the table. Excited cries from the street below, and even the rattle of another engine which seemed to turn a corner and pass suddenly out of hearing, failed to disturb them.

They had been in the room altogether

nearly an hour and a half, and it was by common consent time for them to get back to Old College Street, before she paused again to glance out of the window.

'You can smell it strongly from here, Hal.'

'Ah, the wharves,' he said sagely; 'the wind's that way, you see,'—after a pause of infinitesimal embarrassment—'all there is of it.'

She stood for two seconds before the window-sill with the measure in her hand, musing as if in doubt, and resumed more quickly, 'Oh yes, I think that'll be the very thing. Now we really must be——Hal, what's that funny white stuff falling? *It looks like snow.*'

Long, long, did Walford remember how the tinkle of those trivial words had rung up the curtain on the great tragedy of their lives.

Snow does not usually fall in early autumn even in Great Britain. Was that why his face turned the colour of the two or three fragments of ash, one the size of half a postage stamp, that fluttered into the room and fell upon the dark tablecloth under the lamp?

Then suddenly the noise down in the street seemed to become louder. Far below them, somewhere on the lowest floors of St. Michael's

Mansions, there was a stampede of feet, and a heavy door banged with a thunderous clang that reverberated up the well. And then above other noises rose a cry—the scream of a woman's voice, abject and terrified, no mere sensational outcry, but one of those personally addressed appeals that cleave a man's life into two clean halves: *Fire! Fy-ah!! Fah-eer!!!*

At the same instant a brazen drum down in Catchbrook Street seemed to strike up a sort of muffled alarum, and before three of its panting pulsations had echoed up the walls, Walford realised that the 'Mansions' were well alight, and that one engine had already got to work in front of the house.

Cursing his own negligence, he flew to the inner door, to find the lobby wreathed with smoke. He flung wide the close-fitting outer door, and there rolled in, not wreaths, but volumes, dense and dark, streaming up from below. He craned over the stair-rail and looked down as well as he might through the stifling cloud. From the lower floors came a dull, roaring sound that seemed to stop the very motion of his heart. He ran down to the next landing; there he could hardly face the smoke, and the heat was already alarming. The roar of a conflagration below grew louder ; he could even make sure that the noise came chiefly from the warehouse at the back. It must then have been on fire for some time, and have burnt sideways into the Mansions. On that side, he reflected, was the hydraulic lift. The iron balustrade was warm to the hand, and long tongues of flame flashed up here and there through the blinding waves, which now compelled him to beat a hasty retreat. The well was beginning to draw like a blast furnace.

'Ten minutes ago!' he gasped to himself, as he darted up the stairs. Ten minutes ago, perhaps, one man wrapped in a few yards of sopping blanket might have dared the rush downstairs—*perhaps;* but now, and with her to think of, it was beyond dreaming.

A few steps below the top he found her, half-leaning, half-crouching against the rail, sick with terror of the height and of the flames below; her black hair dishevelled and blacker than ever against her blanched cheeks, and the lustre gone from her eyes.

'Can't we get down?' she cried to him in a faint voice, struggling with her fear.

'Impossible,' he panted shortly, raising and almost carrying her inside the flat, while he slammed the door heavily with his back. 'Don't be frightened,' he added, settling her on the sofa; 'they 've got an engine or two to work, and an escape will be here in two minutes, only we must let them know.'

He put his head out of the window, and yelled lustily, '*Help!—help!—stair—case—on fire—woman—here,*' and, after a pause, '*the—long—escape—quick!*'

The newly invented American 'Telescope,' as the men called it, recurred to his mind. 'That,' he thought to himself, 'would get us down, and it 's about the only chance.'

Perhaps it was. At that very moment a family of children were spinning down it, one after another, from the top story of a house in South London.

But a fireman below, staring a bit, made answer, making a speaking trumpet of his hands while he shoved across the roadway with his booted feet a palpitating python-coil of hose, from which the spray squirted at every crack some thirty feet into the air. 'All right,' he shouted, 'Bill 's got 'er . . . easy there!'—

as another pair of foaming horses trampled and splashed the broad and shallow rapid coursing down the kennel, and the sucker of a third engine was hurled into the boiling dam,—'Stand by, below there! *Ah-h-h! my Lord!*'

Walford, unable to distinguish the words addressed to him, looked straight down below his window, and saw a sight of terror. There was a woman imprisoned on the fourth floor, to which a ladder had been reared that fell short by some ten feet of the window at which she stood leaning half out, afraid to retreat, for the flames were close behind her, and afraid to fall. The ladder seemed almost erect against the wall. But 'Bill' was a hero, though accident or the stress of circumstances provided him with such poor resources for action.

'Let yerself drop, mum,' he cried hoarsely to the wizened elderly female trembling above him.

'No, no,' shrieked Walford, momentarily absorbed in a more acute peril than his own. 'No, no, wait; get a rope up.'

Half-giddy with fear, the woman sprang, instead of falling; it was but a little, but that was enough. The man leant back to catch her; these gymnastics were all part of the day's work to him. With a catlike effort he grasped the falling bundle of clothes, locked his feet in the rungs of the ladder, and stiffened his back to break the blow. Probably he knew by that fraction of a second that all was over. The top of the miserable ladder leapt out from the wall, balanced for the space of half a breath, quivered, undulated, and fell backwards with a crash on to the pavement.

Walford shut his eyes, till a groan of horror from the street, audible above the drumming of three engines, the stamping of horses, and the cries of men, concluded the agonising suspense. The whole scene had not occupied two minutes.

'Poor man!' moaned the crowd. 'His wife, p'raps . . . or his mother.'

He turned back into the room. The girl flew towards him.

'No, no,' he cried, embracing her. 'Don't look out, it's too . . . don't be frightened, darling. There's been an accident!'

He looked out again himself and called. The crowd were making a lane for something carried away on a stretcher. He paused and called again. . . . An answer came up, in which the word 'wait' was distinguishable, but lacking that robust assurance which one on whom the claws and teeth of mortal danger are leisurely closing likes to hear from a rescuer.

There was a minute of maddening interval, during which Walford—the girl helping him, like one in a dream—collected blankets and sheets from the bedroom and soused them with water. Having done it, as there seemed no other use for the apparatus he heaped it up against the outer door, under and around which the smoke was now being forced in fine dark swirls like curling black hair. Such activity merely occupied the hands, while his brain seemed to be racing like a weaver's shuttle, spinning that warp of useless 'whys' which, crossed with the woof of unanswerable 'hows,' soon makes up the web of despair. 'Why had no proper fire-escape arrived? Why had the men only ladders, and ladders which were too short?' All actual recent shortcomings, all the complaints he could recall being hurled at the Brigade, flashed through his mind; how, on quite a recent occasion, the only accessible escape had been found padlocked, and the key (safe in the pocket of an absent custodian) not found at all; or, again, how casual diners-out had made mirth of the new superintendent as one who indeed destroyed less of valuable property, but put out fewer fires than his popular predecessor. He caught himself half-smiling, lost in a wild momentary reverie, from which the sharp, imperious 'toot-toot' of a steam-whistle awoke him. 'Signal,' thought Walford,—'putting another length on one of the hoses up in Catchbrook Street.'

In fact, from the top windows of the side street round the corner a veritable flood was being poured upon the now blazing wing of the Mansions. Nevertheless, the particular engineer with his hand on that shrieking valve was one of the body encamped in Gloria Road, around whom a dark hedge of stalwart and serious police kept off the struggling and yelling crowd; and he was looking up at Walford's window. And Walford, mechanically donning the helmet which lay on the table, attended to his call obediently as a fireman balanced on some roof-top to the familiar note which warns him that the leaping and pulsating monster his arms can hardly direct will next minute be an inanimate log with a decided 'list' streetwards.

He looked out, leant out, and distinctly heard a final answer from a superior official in uniform, who shouted calmly and, as it seemed, desperately. The girl within, from the sofa at which she knelt unseen, heard him mention two Parliamentary divisions of the metropolis, Amberwell and North Brislington, and, a second or two later, during momentary cessations of the turmoil below, had learned the worst. 'The roof at the back . . . a rope over . . . that's all you can do . . . perhaps in twenty minutes.'

She had risen trembling, before Walford turned his white face back into the room.

'What is it?' she asked idly, with pursed and quivering lips.

'Come along,' a strangely faint voice answered. 'We must get on the leads.'

* * * * *

It was now dark, but the swelling crowd in the street, impelled by curiosity or the blind passion that for centuries peopled the amphitheatres, pressed heavily and vociferously upon the living barrier that girt the 'laager' of the Fire Brigade. The sensation-craving attitude of the vulgar herd on such occasions is, as a rule, but little akin to sympathy. Within the limits of a peril which does not approach the uncontrollable, or involve the actual destruction of lives, it verges rather upon an indifference to everything but the prolongation of the display. Not for nothing have imaginative nations worshipped fire, 'a fetich at once so simple and sublime that all productions of the chisel paled before it.' But to-night the sense of impending tragedy seemed to weigh heavily upon all spectators, active and passive, and found expression in a vast hoarse murmur, that only now and then broke up into discordant cries. Among the besieging force, short of numbers, resources, and supplies—a hose-van had come in with the news that official coal would be unreliable for the next hour or so, and long before midnight householders and caretakers of Gloria Road were bringing out their domestic stores in baskets—was a scene of frantic activity, hoarse voices and straining nerves, of which the whole ardour, impatience, and furious energy seemed embodied in each of the seven steamers, whose pantings, like those of fifty brazen-throated Perillus bulls, re-echoed from wall to wall of the wide thoroughfare.

Beneath each gleaming furnace, rocking on its locked wheels, steadily grew and fell away the same pile of blood-red cinders. Above each straining funnel hurtled up into the night the same fierce jets of flame. The whole level street, doubly dark against the light above, was a lagoon dotted with muddy and trampled islands, a marsh about which wallowed in every direction the quaking and bursting coils of hose, like monsters in primæval slime. But on every dripping fold and every muddy pool there flashed now and again rays of crimson and gold from the fires bursting out of all the central windows of the doomed building. Steadily they spread downwards, as blazing rafters and furniture crashed from floor to floor, and rapidly upwards, as after each crash huge tongues and volumes of the fire leapt up with a shriek and a roar, that drew an involuntary responsive murmur from the hundreds of hungry-eyed gazers. And in the distance was audible at intervals the noise of all London, as it seemed, rushing to see the great fire.

To the chief, just arrived on his rounds, and anxiously glancing up at the iron framework (now rapidly being stripped to the bone) of the 'fire-proof' Mansions, a grave-eyed officer of nautical build was curtly explaining the situation.

The warehouse, a huge building stuffed with inflammable material, of which only one (and the smallest) side abutted upon Catchbrook Street, had had an hour's start, or something like it. The fire had begun at a point some twenty yards removed from the street, at the back of this right wing of the Mansions, into which it had burnt deeply before they (the narrator and his friends) had had a call. There was a hope of saving the left wing. 'And we 've lost two lives, one of our——'

'Yes, I heard,' said the chief. 'That was bad.' He bit his grizzled moustachios, and there was pain in his eyes.

'And we 'll lose two more if we don't——'

'Where?' said the superior sharply.

'Top window, left wing, this near side. There, sir, you can see the girl. If we don't get the South Street escape in a quarter of an hour——' He broke off. 'Who's to get at 'em? We 're short of everything 'cept water,' and he glanced at the rapid coursing over his feet.

'That's in use,' said the chief; 'small fire, top floor. Lord Camptown's in Granville Square.'

'Granville Square,' muttered the man. 'Lord! what a night!'

The chief had not taken his eyes from Walford's windows.

'There's a man up there,' he said; 'I saw his helmet.'

The official uttered an execration expressive of surprise.

'That'll be one of Birkett's team . . . they must have got a ladder up at the back . . . or Birkett himself, I'll lay a wager; that chap'd go anywhere.'

'Well, I suppose you'll manage it somehow,' said the superior, with an accent of reassurance. 'I must be off north. You'll have the first four engines I can spare; and mind,' he half turned back on his heel, 'I wouldn't give those second-floor girders another ten minutes—they're pulling in now; that wall will fall outwards. Get your men away.' And he was gone.

The person addressed cast one more glance up at the window on the seventh story; but no figure was visible there, and the whole top floor was beginning to be obscured by the smoke pouring out of the lower windows and rolling along the roof. A light wind had risen and was fanning the flames in that direction.

The corner of the building between the side and main streets exhibited immediately before his eyes a sufficiently wondrous and alarming spectacle. To him it merely represented a trying but interesting crisis in the night-long engagement. The towering angle of the Mansions was thickly wrapped and swathed almost to the summit in shaggy folds of coal-black smoke that hung and gathered like a dense growth of ivy on some ancient turret, and through which ever and anon snapped and flashed darts and volleys of angry flame, like musketry from an embrasure; and as from pavement, window, and roof the glittering torrents of water crashed in in reply, clouds of shrieking steam boiled up into the air and showed huge white blossoms against the murky wreaths that covered the quaking wall. Suddenly the wild, unearthly 'Yahoo!' of a siren sounded over the roofs from the direction of the river.

'The large float,' he said to himself, 'droppin' down to Amberwell; that'll maybe let loose another steamer for this job.'

A grimy salvage man with a bandaged hand, his stalwart form literally besprinkled with mud and ashes, ran by.

'Birkett's got up an escape at the back. Those —— fools broke the other turning a corner. He's brought down a woman.'

'That's all right,' said the man in charge. 'Below there, Simmons!'

An avalanche of charred and blazing timbers fell on the pavement.

* * * * *

Walford grasped Nellie's arm, and together they stumbled through a stifling cloud up the little staircase with an oppressively intense consciousness that a hundred years ago, in a remote sphere of existence, they had gone through an exactly similar process, which was somehow more real than the present. To her indeed the delusion was less actual, for when they reached the roof she collapsed an unconscious burden into his ready arms. Wildly he looked about for a spot of temporary safety and shelter during this fatal delay. He could not leave her reclined against the outer balustrade, for sheets of smoke seemed drifting up the wall from the lower windows. Hastily he scrambled, holding her in one arm, over a ledge of lead, and reached a secluded spot behind a huge stack of chimneys, some yards further from the nearest signs of fire. Here they were within but a few paces of the crevasse-like passage which separated the burning wing of the Mansions from that beyond, deserted in the last half-hour by its few alarmed denizens on the ground floor, but presenting to Walford's eyes the nearest refuge, if it could be reached.

With this reflection in his mind he had dashed back across the leads and down the stairs, fighting his way this time through the smoke which surged up from the lift well. To judge from the smell and the heat, the outer door and the flooring of the bedroom were already smouldering. He seized a jug of water, and having found a flask of brandy, and, as an afterthought, hastily stuffed a few valuables of small compass into his pockets, fled back across the roof. To his inexpressible relief he found her sitting up, white and tear-stained, on a grimy ledge below the chimney-stack.

'I'm all right,' she said, struggling after a respectable bravery. 'I think it was the smoke. Where have you been, Hal? When will they come and fetch us?'

For all answer he pressed some brandy to her lips, and then pointed across the dark gorge in front of them.

'It's not far,' he said; 'only on to that other roof. The men will be there soon with ropes and a ladder.'

Twenty minutes, he thought to himself, must have elapsed, but what was the help promised in twenty minutes? He had not distinctly heard—was it the American fire-escape, or what? Further communication with the street was impossible. He turned and looked back, the girl following his eyes. From the whole area of roof behind them, on two sides, rose a seething wave of fire and smoke that rolled steadily towards them. It was only a matter of time now. The hostile breeze had freshened, and a hot draught met him everywhere as he hastily explored in the failing light all accessible tracts of the roof.

'Wait here a moment, darling,' he said, 'while I look round and see if there is no other way down.'

These indeed were idle words, but he meant to make surer the assurance of rescue by showing himself at some point on the roof. In a few minutes he returned, satisfied that those in the street had seen him. So he said. In his heart he doubted whether, at that height, through the gathering darkness, he could have been discernible. No matter: his first appeal had reached them. No thought of the dress and arms which, by the merest coincidence, he was wearing, and of the delusive significance these might have to professional eyes, disturbed his fatal confidence that the helplessness of their position must be at once realised—that some adequate force would come to the rescue of two innocent beings imprisoned on an islet in the skies and driven towards the abyss by a tidal wave of fire. But the delay was incomprehensible. As the murky pall of smoke rolled up and mingled with the blackness of night, the horror of a deadly isolation seemed to brood over them.

* * * * *

A week's agony—the agony of a siege where relief is despaired of and life failing day by day—compressed into ten minutes, crushed down all instinctive struggles of hope against hope, as the leaden darkness seemed to press down upon them, and the advancing flames drove them towards the black and terrible precipice beyond which lay their only safety. It was impossible they could be seen now, except against or amidst the sheets of flame whose hot breath now and again swept round them—except, that was, from a point from which none were looking, or at a moment when the long-delayed rescue would be of no avail.

* * * * *

He could not have told how long it was after this reflection occurred to him—so swiftly time spun the web of terror round them—that the situation in a flash loomed definitely fatal. He could see flames streaming from the staircase by which they had twice ascended. The rooms in which they had sat and trifled an hour ago, and those adjoining them, now formed an extended wing of the general conflagration, cutting off all approach (had that been of any use) to the wall fronting Gloria Road. Some thirty yards away on the other side, the warehouse—four stories, with all the roof fallen in—roared to heaven in a vast cloud of flame, which shut out all view in that direction, and made their voices scarcely audible to one another. Immediately behind them the first high ridge of chimney-stacks stood out a jetty black against the seething waves and forked tongues of flame that, fanned by the freshening breeze, steadily clutched and devoured the mainland of roof.

Walford was no hero. He had played tentatively with danger, with the half-pleasure of wrestling with the untried and little known. But at this crisis, when the blind horror of death seemed to be engulfing not only life, but all the happiness that could fill it, he felt its cowing, cold-blooded mastery. Yet absolute surrender was impossible while she still lay there, white, helpless, but patient, she whom he had lured up to this hideous height that they might perish together unnoticed in its stupendous holocaust. He leant far over the parapet uttering frenzied cries. He paced backwards and forwards wildly measuring the breadth of the gulf. He climbed upon some raised partition in the roof, and gazed into the depth, imagination and reason racing in his brain, while the fire roared in his ears, for a mortal or miraculous solution of the insoluble problem. 'O for a ladder!' (and despairing fancy mocked him with the echo, 'O for wings!') 'O for a rope!' ('O for an angel from heaven!') The one seemed now as likely to arrive as the other. But then the more bitter reflection forced itself sharply upon his desperate reverie: 'What was to be done here with a rope or ladder?' He could take her in his arms and carry her—but could he carry her? Could he walk twenty feet on the rungs of a horizontal ladder, swaying like a withy, when the slightest false step meant to be dashed to pieces—and he shuddered to think of what he had seen in Gloria Road—upon the pavement below? Could he watch her crawling, struggling across that fearful abyss? He peered down into the darkness below, dotted by a few tiny gas-lamps. In his weakness he almost wished it could be all over at once—for himself . . . but for *her*? A gust of new energy and higher courage shook him like a storm at the thought. It was not their love or happiness, but her life alone that was now to be fought for. He would have a few words yet with the Spectre of Despair. At that moment a red-hot wire struck him smartly in the back.

Looking up, he saw towering above him an object familiar indeed to his eye, but worth description to a reader unacquainted with the monstrosities of a modern capital.

From a point on the roof, about fifteen or twenty feet back from the wall, rose a huge mast some forty feet in height, surmounted by a spire, and supported by stays of iron wire from various parts of the building. Across the upper half of it were fastened, one below another and about a foot apart, some dozen stout cross-bars of wood five or six feet in length. On each bar were fixed half a dozen large earthenware 'insulators,' and the whole framework—which now, with smoke-clouds rolling about it, resembled the mast and rigging of a burning vessel—supported a hundred telephone wires.

'Wait! wait!' shrieked Walford nonsensically enough, with a wild light in his eyes, vaguely fearful that his past antics might have robbed the girl of her last scrap of self-control. 'Wait!' he forced his voice through the hoarse murmurs of rushing flame and the fainter tumult from the streets—' I see!'

She did not, and indeed at first thought him mad, as, unbuttoning his axe and pulling tighter the buckle of his helmet, he rushed to the foot of the gigantic telephone pole, measuring the height to the first crossbar, and then back to the passage, anxiously scanning its width. But what could she do? Nothing. 'Sit still till I call,' he thundered, 'there, right under the parapet, close as you can get.'

Twenty, thirty, forty times did she hear the sound of the axe swung with hearty goodwill upon that stout Norwegian pine. Then he strode towards her again. His voice had a different accent, a touch of the agonised bitterness of a relapse into despair. 'Half the wires are down,' he said, 'and one of the back supports; I can't get at the other.'

Flames surrounded it and drove him back. Indeed, the foot of the pole itself was blackened on the far side, and a rain of sparks drove past it.

He groaned aloud. 'Water, water!'

''Arf a minute, mate!' sounded a stentorian voice from the opposite roof.

Walford turned as if at a shot. The short, squab figure of a Wapping mariner, clad in a dark-blue uniform, carrying in one hand a heavy and gleaming musquetoon, and closely followed by an anaconda of fabulous length, appeared against the skyline. The splendid dawn of the conflagration flashed a quite celestial brightness upon his brass buttons, his red nose, and even the thick wedding-ring on his left hand.

''Arf a minute!' he grunted in the same level tone; 'one long and two short is Jumbo's ticket, and when you 'ear that I'll give you all the water she can send up.' He adjusted the musquetoon in both arms, casting an eagle eye over the territory to be attacked.

'Hello! 'ow will you get the lydy over?' He spoke as if the interval between them were a streamlet in which she might wet her feet.

'All right,' answered Walford with a half-hysterical yell, 'we're coming across directly. Put that hose on me.' And then a long, piercing wail from the depths below, followed with breathless rapidity by two stifled shrieks that stuck in the ear like darts, wiped out the rest of his exclamation as a sponge wipes out the writing on a slate. He pointed to a skylight or trap from which flames were beginning to stream up and play round the base of the mast, like some bright-coloured creeper feeling for a support.

'Lay down.'

As the black coils behind him heaved and stiffened, the man chucked the words at Walford like a four of bricks. He lay down on his elbows, till a passing douche from the hose directed on to the leads just in front of him drove all the breath out of his body, and almost lifted it into the air. Recovering, he staggered back, axe in hand, through the shower of sparks, and in a moment was desperately at work again. Two feet to one side of him the rigid glistening torrent hung and thundered with an explosion of hisses into the burning aperture in the roof. The mightier waves of the fire beyond made the surging roar of a stormy sea. The sound of blows was audible above it. As the current first wavered, Walford looked up, shaking a red ash from his sleeve. The fireman was addressing him, but he could only hear part of his remarks.

''Ow did yer get up? . . . ain't no use . . . fix up this a bit, and go fetch . . .'

He shook his head, and bellowed back grotesque and disjointed replies. 'I'm not a fireman. Keep on a minute,' and a second later, as he stooped over the iron stay, 'Your axe, quick!'

It was bowled over adroitly. Walford deliberately chipped its edge against the side of his own, and in a trice was at work filing the twisted iron wire. The sweat poured over him and dripped upon the leads like rain, yet still he worked on. Three minutes passed, and the squab, red-nosed man, who had been murmuring to himself, 'I'm not a fireman! Then 'oo the doose in all might you be?' beginning to fear that he had to do with some one naturally lunatic, or deranged by the terror of the catastrophe, began to protest in his own language. With face rubicund as the flames that illumined it, he implored Walford (who had begun again) to leave off chopping at a sanguinary pole which wasn't in the way, and must clearly (whatever happened) be burnt in another quarter of an hour. To his despair, the lunatic, whom he now began to regard as dangerous, continued to dance about, axe in hand, in a state apparently of mingled exultation and indignation.

'Nellie,' he shrieked hoarsely, 'get out of the way, there, to the left!' and to the thunder-struck man from Wapping, 'Shut up, you —— fool! Now, then! it's coming down! mind yourself!'

There was a sudden crack as of a rotten forest tree struck and felled by an October gale, and the inevitable, which was also the astonishing, had once more come to pass.

Of the one hundred and eight telephone wires, a great number had already subsided, in a more or less liquefied state, into the huge furnace over which they had stretched. The stays on the further side being cut away, and the timber itself half-severed, the strain of the unbroken wires or supports brought the whole framework down at right angles across the wall and the passage. The virtue of this operation of the law of gravity lay in the simple fact that the distance of the base of the mast from the first crossbar and from the wall was about the same, in which coincidence also was nothing remarkable. But when an unearthly discharge of grape and canister in the form of flying insulators and broken shards of earthenware had smashed the windows and starred the pavement a hundred feet below, it became apparent that there lay across the dreaded gulf, like a drawbridge unexpectedly let down from the skies, a solid causeway, across which four men abreast might easily walk with no possibility of falling through, and even a small vehicle might have been driven.

At the sight of this dangerous miracle, the man from Wapping dropped his hose and fled. Cautiously returning, he kicked aside the broken spire and grasped the new structure to test its solidity. As there seemed no likelihood of its moving further, he nodded in a reassuring manner to the two figures advancing towards him, blackly silhouetted against the background of fire.

With a frenzied light of triumph in his eye, Walford himself tramped upon the first cross-bar to be sure that this wondrous inspiration would not vanish back into the fairyland of fancy from which it had so swiftly been bodied forth. But all was not ready yet. Although many of the broken wires had fallen, dragged down into the street, and disappeared, a bosky tangle lay about the level roof and cumbered the cause-way. One or two had even entangled the girl and charred her dress, till the hose once more swept across them and left only a steaming briary tangle in their path. This Walford hastened with wild fury to trample down or sweep aside, cutting off some of the obstructive strands and catching others round the crossbars. His hands were burnt and blackened. The hot blast pressed on them from behind, but like a solid marble handrail the gleaming column of water from the hose stood by their sides, and hurtled past them into the advancing wing of the fire. There was yet time. Then he turned and said simply, ‘Come along . . . come along . . . like that . . . step on the bars, not on the pole . . . because they ’re flat . . . from one to the other. . . .’

But the transit was not to be hastily accomplished. It was a condensed deliberate agony of stumbles and struggles,—a passage to be remembered, as a man remembers his first rough week in the Bay of Biscay. And just as they reached the middle of the gulf, a long, grinding roar shook the building behind and the bridge beneath them. Crouching down, they both clutched at the trembling woodwork till the shock passed by, and the thunderous noise died down into a distant chorus of cries and the rustling as of a mighty wind just getting up. At the same moment, a new and towering aurora of light filled the sky behind, and threw the black outline of their two figures, and the brushwood of telephone wires about them, half on the crossbars, and half on the opposite wall below.

'All right, sir; all right, lady,' cried a husky but cheering voice. 'Thet's the far wall come down.' And so it was.

Arrived on the shore of safety in a kind of dream, Walford's first act was to shake hands warmly with the red-nosed man.

'You ain't a fireman!' ejaculated the latter, adding with a sledge-hammer emphasis as he resumed his hose, '*Golly!*'

* * * * *

Not till they had descended into the street were they clear of dreamland. Then first could the mind, gradually permeated by the body's enjoyment of the safe and solid earth, make up its actual account with happiness. It was he, of course, who made the first pretence of a recovery, propounding in a voice carefully modelled after his own the original inquiry, 'How are you?'

For answer, the colour slowly returned to her cheeks, and cautiously, as if fearful of rousing the jealousy of an eluded fate, she broke into a tearful smile at the singularity of her appearance leaning on the arm of a figure still dripping with water, his clothes torn and blackened with the grime of the roof. Then stopping for a minute, with hands that still trembled, she put back her wandering black hair into something like presentable tidiness.

* * * * *

The events above described had not disturbed the serenity of the little *cul-de-sac* known as 'Old College Street.' Arrived hurriedly upstairs, and there beset by a torrent of obvious questions, Walford, while a belated supper was preparing, led the anxious mother to the window of her back drawing-room, and drew up the blind. Beyond the first low roofs, a vast volcano flared to heaven. 'There,' he said, before the speechless lady could articulate another inquiry, 'that 's St. Michael's Mount . . . and Nellie 's rather tired, and I 'm a bit wet and dirty. Nothing more.'

'The heroism and the presence of mind, not to say astonishing ingenuity, of one member of the brigade in particular, which will, we trust, be rewarded by some adequate testimonial,' was belauded in several leading articles of the next morning. But the writers who penned these eulogies knew not that they were but celebrating one more manifestation of that which the Greek poet had long ago described as equal to all forces of Nature and all emergencies—of 'Love unconquered in fight.' The hero, indeed, met, according to his own account, with an adequate reward; but it did not take the form of a public testimonial.

'According to that theory'—said a critical friend, *à propos* of the last story but one—'susceptibility of "discipline" would be the chief test of animal character, which means that the best dogs get their character from men. If so——'

'You pity the poor brutes?'

'Oh no. I was going to say that on that principle cats should have next to no character at all.'

'They have plenty,' I said, 'but it's usually bad—at least, hopelessly unromantic. Who ever heard of a heroic or self-denying cat? Cats do what they like, not what you want them to do.'

He laughed. 'Sometimes they do what you like very much. You haven't heard Mrs. Warburton-Kinneir's cat-story?'

'The Warburton-Kinneirs! I didn't know they were back in England.'

'Oh yes. They've been six months in Hampshire, and now they are in town. She has Thursday afternoons.'

'Good,' I said. 'I'll go the very next Friday, and take my chance. . . .'

Fortunately only one visitor appeared to tea. And as soon as I had explained my curiosity, he joined me in petitioning for the story which follows:—

*　　*　　*　　*　　*

Stoffles was her name, a familiar abbreviation, and Mephistophelian was her nature. She had all the usual vices of the feline tribe, including a double portion of those which men are so fond of describing as feminine. Vain, indolent, selfish, with a highly cultivated taste for luxury and neatness in her personal appearance, she was distinguished by all those little irritating habits and traits for which nothing but an affectionate heart (a thing in her case conspicuous by its absence) can atone.

It would be incorrect, perhaps, to say that Stoffles did not care for the society of my husband or myself. She liked the best of everything, and these our circumstances allowed us to give her. For the rest, though in kitten days suspected of having caught a mouse, she had never been known in after life to do anything which the most lax of economists could describe as useful. She would lie all day in the best armchair enjoying real or pretended slumbers, which never affected her appetite at supper-time; although in that eventide which is the feline morn she would, if certain of a sufficient number of admiring spectators, condescend to amuse their dull human intelligence by exhibitions of her dexterity. But she was soon bored, and had no conception of altruistic effort. Abundantly cautious and prudent in all matters concerning her own safety and comfort, she had that feline celerity of vanishing like air or water before the foot, hand, or missile of irritated man; while on the other hand, when a sensitive specimen of the gentler sex (my grandmother, for example) was attentively holding the door open for her, she would stiffen and elongate her whole body, and, regardless of all exhibitions of kindly impatience, proceed out of the drawing-room as slowly as a funeral *cortège* of crocodiles.

A good-looking Persian cat is an ornamental

piece of furniture in a house; but though fond of animals, I never succeeded in getting up an affection for Stoffles until the occurrence of the incident here to be related. Even in this, however, I cannot conceal from myself that the share which she took was taken, as usual, solely for her own satisfaction.

We live, you know, in a comfortable old-fashioned house facing the highroad, on the slope of a green hill from which one looked across the gleaming estuary (or the broad mud-flats) of Southampton Water on to the rich, rolling woodland of the New Forest. I say *we*, but in fact for some months I had been alone, and my husband had just returned from one of his sporting and scientific expeditions in South America. He had already won fame as a naturalist, and had succeeded in bringing home alive quite a variety of beasts, usually of the reptile order, whose extreme rarity seemed to me a merciful provision of Nature.

But all his previous triumphs were completely eclipsed, I soon learned, by the capture, alive, on this last expedition, of an abominably poisonous snake, known to those who knew it as the Blue Dryad, or more familiarly, in backwoods slang, as the Half-hour Striker, in vague reference to its malignant and fatal qualities. The time in which a snake-bite takes effect is, by the way, no very exact test of its virulence, the health and condition not only of the victim, but of the snake, having of course to be taken into account.

But the Blue Dryad, sometimes erroneously described as a variety of rattlesnake, is, I understand, supposed to kill the average man, under favourable circumstances, in less time even than the deadly Copperhead—which it somewhat resembles, except that it is larger in size, and bears a peculiar streak of faint peacock-blue down the back, only perceptible in a strong light. This precious reptile was destined for the Zoological Gardens.

Being in extremely delicate health at the time, I need hardly say that I knew nothing of these gruesome details until afterwards. Henry (that is my husband), after entering my room with a robust and sunburned appearance that did my heart good, merely observed—as soon as we had exchanged greetings—that he had brought home a pretty snake which 'wouldn't (just as long, that is to say, as it couldn't) do the slightest harm,'—an evasive assurance which I accepted as became the nervous wife of an enthusiastic naturalist. I believe I insisted on its not coming into the house.

The cook, indeed, on my husband expressing a wish to put it in the kitchen, had taken up a firmer position: she had threatened to 'scream' if 'the vermin' were introduced into her premises; which ultimatum, coming from a stalwart young woman with unimpaired lungs, was sufficient.

Fortunately the weather was very hot (being in July of the ever-memorable summer of 1893), so it was decided that the Blue Dryad, wrapped in flannel and securely confined in a basket, should be left in the sun, and the farthest corner of the verandah, during the hour or so in the afternoon when my husband had to visit the town on business.

He had gone off with a cousin of mine, an officer of Engineers in India, stationed I think at Lahore, and home on leave. I remember that they were a long time, or what seemed to me a long time, over their luncheon; and the last remark of our guest as he came out of the dining-room remained in my head as even meaningless words will run in the head of any idle invalid shut up for most of the day in a silent room. What he said was, in the positive tone of one emphasising a curious and surprising statement, 'D'you know, by the way, it's the *one* animal that doesn't care a rap for the cobra.' And, my husband seeming to express disbelief and a desire to change the subject as they entered my boudoir, 'It's a holy fact! Goes for it, so smart! Has the beggar on toast before you can say "Jack Robinson!"'

The observation did not interest me, but simply ran in my head. Then they came into my room, only for a few moments, as I was not to be tired. The Engineer tried to amuse Stoffles, who was seized with such a fit of mortal boredom that he transferred his attentions to Ruby, the Gordon setter, a devoted and inseparable friend of mine, under whose charge I was shortly left as they passed out of the house. The Lieutenant, it appears, went last, and inadvertently closed without fastening the verandah door. Thereby hangs a tale of the most trying quarter of an hour it has been my lot to experience.

I suppose I may have been asleep for ten minutes or so when I was awakened by the noise of Ruby's heavy body jumping out through the open window. Feeling restless and seeing me asleep, he had imagined himself entitled to a short spell off guard. Had the door not been ostensibly latched he would have made his way out by it, being thoroughly used to opening doors and such tricks—a capacity which in fact proved fatal to him. That it was unlatched I saw in a few moments, for the dog on his return forced it open with a push and trotted up in a disturbed manner to my bedside. I noticed a tiny spot of blood on the black side of his nose, and naturally supposed he had scratched himself against a bush or a piece of wire. 'Ruby,' I said, 'what have you been doing?' Then he whined as if in pain, crouching close to my side and shaking in every limb. I should say that I was myself lying with a shawl over my feet on a deep sofa with a high back. I turned to look at Stoffles, who was slowly perambulating the room, looking for flies and other insects (her favourite amusement) on the wainscot. When I glanced again at the dog his appearance filled me with horror ; he was standing, obviously from pain, swaying from side to side and breathing hard. As I watched, his body grew more and more rigid. With his eyes fixed on the half-open door, he drew back as if from the approach of some dreaded object, raised his head with a pitiful attempt at a bark, which broke off into a stifled howl, rolled over sideways suddenly, and lay dead. The horrid stiffness of the body, almost resembling a stuffed creature overset, made me believe that he had died as he stood, close to my side, perhaps meaning to defend me—more probably, since few dogs would be proof against such a terror, trusting that I should protect him against the *thing coming in at the door!* Unable to resist the unintelligible idea that the dog had been frightened to death, I followed the direction of his last gaze, and at first saw nothing. The next moment I observed round the corner of the verandah door a small, dark, and slender object, swaying gently up and down like a dry bough in the wind. It had passed right into the room with the same slow, regular motion before I realised what it was and what had happened.

My poor, stupid Ruby must have nosed at

the basket on the verandah till he succeeded somehow in opening it, and have been bitten in return for his pains by the abominable beast which had been warranted in this insufficient manner to do no harm, and which I now saw angrily rearing its head and hissing fiercely at the dead dog within three yards of my face.

I am not one of those women who jump on chairs or tables when they see a mouse, but I have a constitutional horror of the most harmless reptiles. Watching the Blue Dryad as it glided across the patch of sunlight streaming in from the open window, and knowing what it was, I confess to being as nearly frightened out of my wits as I ever hope to be. If I had been well, perhaps I might have managed to scream and run away. As it was, I simply dared not speak or move a finger for fear of attracting the beast's attention to myself. Thus I remained a terrified spectator of the astonishing scene which followed. The whole thing seemed to me like a dream. As the beast entered the room, I seemed again to hear my cousin making the remark above mentioned about the cobra. *What* animal, I wondered dreamily, could he have meant? Not Ruby! Ruby was dead. I looked at his stiff body again, and shuddered. The whistle of a train sounded from the valley below, and then an errand-boy passed along the road at the back of the house (for the second or third time that day) singing in a cracked voice the fragment of a popular melody, of which I am sorry to say I know no more—

> 'I've got a little cat,
> And I'm very fond of that;
> But daddy wouldn't buy me a bow, wow, wow';

the *wow-wows* becoming fainter and further as the youth strode down the hill. If I had been 'myself,' as the poor folk say, this coincidence would have made me laugh, for at that very moment Stoffles, weary of patting flies and spiders on the back, appeared gently purring on the crest, so to speak, of the sofa.

It has often occurred to me since that if the scale of things had been enlarged—if Stoffles, for example, had been a Bengal tiger, and the Dryad a boa-constrictor or crocodile,—the tragedy which followed would have been worthy of the pen of any sporting and dramatic historian. I can only say that, being transacted in such objectionable proximity to myself, the thing was as impressive as any combat of mastodon and iguanodon could have been to primitive man.

Stoffles, as I have said, was inordinately vain and self-conscious. Stalking along the top of the sofa-back and bearing erect the bushy banner of her magnificent tail, she looked the most ridiculous creature imaginable. She had proceeded half-way on this pilgrimage towards me when suddenly, with the rapidity of lightning, as her ear caught the sound of the hiss and her eyes fell upon the Blue Dryad, her whole civilised 'play-acting' demeanour vanished, and her body stiffened and contracted to the form of a watchful wild beast with the ferocious and instinctive antipathy to a natural enemy blazing from its eyes. No change of a shaken kaleidoscope could have been more complete or more striking. In one light bound she was on the floor in a compressed, defensive attitude, with all four feet close together, near, but not too near, the unknown but clearly hostile intruder; and to my surprise, the snake turned and made off towards the window. Stoffles trotted lightly after, obviously interested in its method of locomotion. Then she made a long arm and playfully dropped a paw upon its tail. The snake wriggled free in a moment, and coiling its whole length, some three and a half feet, fronted this new and curious antagonist.

At the very first moment, I need hardly say, I expected that one short stroke of that little pointed head against the cat's delicate body would quickly have settled everything. But one is apt to forget that a snake (I suppose because in romances snakes always 'dart') can move but slowly and awkwardly over a smooth surface, such as a tiled or wooden floor. The long body, in spite of its wonderful construction, and of the attitudes in which it is frequently drawn, is no less subject to the laws of gravitation than that of a hedgehog. A snake that 'darts' when it has nothing secure to hold on by, only overbalances itself. With half or two-thirds of the body firmly coiled against some rough object or surface, the head —of a poisonous snake at least—is indeed a deadly weapon of precision. This particular reptile, perhaps by some instinct, had now wriggled itself on to a large and thick fur rug about twelve feet square, upon which arena took place the extraordinary contest that followed.

The audacity of the cat astonished me from the first. I have no reason to believe she had ever seen a snake before, yet by a sort of instinct she seemed to know exactly what she was doing. As the Dryad raised its head, with glittering eyes and forked tongue, Stoffles crouched with both front paws in the air, sparring as I had seen her do sometimes with a large moth. The first round passed so swiftly that mortal eye could hardly see with distinctness what happened. The snake made a dart, and the cat, all claws, two rapid blows at its advancing head. The first missed, but the second I could see came home, as the brute, shaking its neck and head, withdrew further into the jungle—I mean, of course, the rug. But Stoffles, who had no idea of the match ending in this manner, crept after it, with an air of attractive carelessness which was instantly rewarded. A full two feet of the Dryad's body straightened like a black arrow, and seemed to strike right into the furry side of its antagonist—seemed, I say, to slowgoing human eyes; but the latter shrank, literally *fell* back, collapsing with such suddenness that she seemed to have turned herself inside out, and become the mere skin of a cat. As the serpent recovered itself, she pounced on it like lightning, driving at least half a dozen claws well home, and then, apparently realising that she had not a good enough hold, sprang lightly into the air from off the body, alighting about a yard off. There followed a minute of sparring in the air; the snake seemingly half afraid to strike, the cat waiting on its every movement.

Now the poisonous snake when provoked is an irritable animal, and the next attack of the Dryad, maddened by the scratchings of puss and its own unsuccessful exertions, was so furious, and so close to myself, that I shuddered for the result. Before this stage I might perhaps, with a little effort, have escaped, but now panic fear glued me to the spot; indeed, I could not have left my position on the sofa without almost treading upon Stoffles, whose bristling back was not a yard from my feet. At last, I thought—as the Blue Dryad, for one second coiled close as a black silk cable, sprang out the next as straight and sharp as the piston-rod of an engine,—this lump of feline vanity and conceit is done for, and—I could not help thinking—it will probably be my turn next! Little did I appreciate the resources of Stoffles, who, without a change in her vigilant pose, without a wink of her fierce green eyes, sprang backwards and upwards on to the top of me and there confronted the enemy calmly as ever, sitting, if you please, upon my feet! I don't know that any gymnastic performance ever surprised me more than this, though I have seen this very beast drop twenty feet from a window-sill on to a stone pavement without appearing to notice any particular change of level. Cats with so much plumage have probably their own reasons for not flying.

Trembling all over with fright, I could not but observe that she was trembling too—with rage. Whether instinct inspired her with the advantages of a situation so extremely unpleasant to me, I cannot say. The last act of the drama rapidly approached, and no more strategic catastrophe was ever seen.

For a snake, as everybody knows, naturally

rears its head when fighting. In that position, though one may hit it with a stick, it is extremely difficult, as this battle had shown, to get hold of. Now, as the Dryad, curled to a capital S, quivering and hissing advanced for the last time to the charge, it was bound to strike across the edge of the sofa on which I lay, at the erect head of Stoffles, which vanished with a juggling celerity that would have dislocated the collar-bone of any other animal in creation. From such an exertion the snake recovered itself with an obvious effort, quick beyond question, but not nearly quick enough. Before I could well see that it had missed its aim, Stoffles had launched out like a spring released, and, burying eight or ten claws in the back of its enemy's head, pinned it down against the stiff cushion of the sofa. The tail of the agonised reptile flung wildly in the air and flapped on the arched back of the imperturbable tigress. The whiskered muzzle of Stoffles dropped quietly, and her teeth met once, twice, thrice, like the needle and hook of a sewing-machine, in the neck of the Blue Dryad; and when, after much deliberation, she let it go, the beast fell into a limp tangle on the floor.

When I saw that the thing was really dead I believe I must have fainted. Coming to myself, I heard hurried steps and voices. 'Great heavens!' my husband was screaming, 'where has the brute got to?' 'It's all right,' said the Engineer; 'just you come and look here, old man. Commend me to the coolness of that cat. After the murder of your priceless specimen, here's Stoffles cleaning her fur in one of her serenest Anglo-Saxon attitudes.'

So she was. My husband looked grave as I described the scene. 'Didn't I tell you so?' said the Engineer, 'and this beast, I take it, is worse than any cobra.'

I can easily believe he was right. From the gland of the said beast, as I afterwards learned, they extracted enough poison to be the death of twenty full-grown human beings.

Tightly clasped between its minute teeth was found (what interested me more) a few long hairs, late the property of Stoffles.

Stoffles, however—she is still with us—has a superfluity of long hair, and is constantly leaving it about.

HOW THE FIEND FETCHED SHARON FULKSAY

A STORY OF THE SUBURBS

TRAVELLERS who often go in and out of London by the Great North Midland Railway are familiar with the name—painted at full length in large letters—of Harnsleigh Grove Park.

It is one of those suburban stations which strike one as hideous monuments erected in memory of deceased 'bits of country,'—alive and green a few years ago, then beslobbered with filth and smoke, and at last bodily devoured by the dragon jaws of the advancing metropolis.

The nomenclature of such districts often seems to represent a frantic struggle on the part of commercial enterprise to make a living 'neighbourhood' out of a mere mechanical congeries of atoms, unwilling residents, bad bricks, gas-lamps, and cheap iron railings.

In the particular case of Harnsleigh Grove Park the senseless conglomeration of substantives, vaguely suggestive of nightingales and greenery, seemed a particularly ghastly irony upon the actual nature of the place, which was a desert of cottage-villas of the dreariest type that ever made an artist weep.

The yellow of its brickwork was more sickly, the meaningless patterns of its front walls more irritating, and its wanton and soulless uniformity more crushing, than those of any other London suburb of similar size.

Within its vast area of gloomy little cells were nightly stowed away, and from them were daily brought forth, thousands upon thousands of small clerks and commercial employés—the trusted and responsible servants, many of them, of great firms and millionaires living in the real 'country,' or the West End. Everybody you saw on the way to or from the station—you could hardly see them anywhere else — presented the same 'machine-turned' type of honesty and industry. Respectability positively 'rampant,' on a ground commonplace, might have stood as the heraldic insignia of the locality. Philanthropic missions and improving lectures flourished like lotteries or variety entertainments elsewhere;

till the rebellious soul of the scoffer could almost have wished an epidemic of iniquity to descend upon the place and confound its wearisome propriety. The immaculate spires of three or four brand-new churches dotted here and there the level growth of villas—like taller plants in a painfully trim garden: churches where cashiers of unimpeachable integrity held the plate, book-keepers of positively reverend respectability dropped in their subscriptions, and industrious clerks of the most regular habits sang in the choir; while their respectable mothers, sisters, and aunts settled, by almost imperceptible distinctions of costume, the nice gradations of respectable suburban society. Generally speaking, these might be taken to comprehend the most exciting questions and interests of the neighbourhood. To the superficial and unprejudiced eye all the inhabitants seemed as methodically regular in character, and as like one another, as their streets and houses.

All the vast army lived the same kind of life, had the same sort of pictures on the walls, the same sort of ornamented cottage piano in the same niche (expressly left, alternately on the right or left of the cottage parlour, by the ingenious wholesale architect), wore the same cut of clothes, the same pattern of tall (or more often round) hat, breakfasted, presumably, at the same uncomfortable hour (the pot-hats, however, preceding the toppers by forty minutes or so), read the same kind of newspapers in the train, and at the huge terminus of the Great North Midland were similarly lost in the vast ocean of 'city traffic' that poured in from a dozen other commercial suburbs.

The brief journey, by the way, from Harnsleigh Grove Park to the metropolis is perhaps more depressing than any pilgrimage of a hundred miles in any other direction.

The route is that one of all others by which London should not be approached, after a six weeks' holiday in the country, by any one not anxious to raise its very creditable death-rate. For, thus viewed, the city is apt to seem a mere hideous and unbearable blot upon the universe.

The line is one of those to which whole streets of the vulgarest houses seem to have turned their backs in disgust. Its perspectives of slum-attics, dirty clothing, and sickly thrushes in small wooden cages are probably unsurpassed in all the capitals of Europe.

The blatant and glaring advertisements, whose numbers and assurance exhibit a conviction that the human horde travelling this defile is their helpless prey, hunt the flagging eye, like wolves, up and down the dreary foreground. But the full effect of the neighbourhood can only be caught when it is traversed slowly on a foggy evening in winter, when every paltry station stands out like a sort of gaslit island or solitary mountain-top rising out of a sea of gloom ; when camp-fires flare along the murky embankment, and the heavy banging, now here and now there, of the explosive signals on the line suggests the idea of a trainful of hostile invaders received by dropping fire from an ambuscade ; when the ruddy clouds of drifting fog surge up round you, lit by a fitful glare from the clamorous streets below, like the smoke of a sacked and burning city ; when, in fine, the Great North Midland Railway presents to every wearied passenger, over and above the legal value of his fare, a very passable conception of the back entrance, if there be such, into the infernal regions.

* * * * *

Travelling through the place by daytime, I was always struck by the appearance of one particular house, which seemed to have been shaved off by the line like a piece of cheese.

The house itself would not have seemed particularly interesting if all of it had been there, or at all remarkable if it had stood in a street of detached villas. But the fact that it actually abutted on—or rather seemed to have been cut in two by—the railway, gave it a sort of character which none of the surroundings had, and amid the spick-and-span villadom of the place it wore the air of an antique and almost venerable 'pile,' being in fact an insignificant specimen of the most debased Georgian architecture. A few trees, including one ragged poplar, and what looked like the gable of a decayed summer-house, were visible over the high wall that skirted the permanent way; and in the middle of the said wall, where it obviously formed a part of the house, was a small round window like a port-hole. From the very first I had an instinctive feeling against the house, a dreamy fancy of some innocent victim imprisoned in the room with the port-hole, or perhaps—this would be on some foggy night—thrust out from it on to the line in the way of an advancing express train.

But while vaguely wondering who lived there, what they did in the dismal bit of garden behind the wall, and how they slept at nights, one had an underlying conviction that nothing of an exciting nature could be connected with a building so essentially commonplace, embedded in the centre of a modern London suburb.

* * * * *

Years afterwards, I paid two or three visits to Harnsleigh Grove Park in connection with the Sunday Suburban Concert Association; and thus, as it seemed, by the merest accident, my curiosity about the place was satisfied.

The romantic imagination of the reader will perhaps have conjured up a vision of stately hall and flowing lawn, feudal splendour and Arcadian loveliness, which had given place to the stern reality of a middle-class building-estate. As a matter of fact, I learned there had been nothing particularly beautiful there for near a century past.

The very core and centre of the place, so to

speak, from which it drew its name, had been an ugly staring manor-house standing in an unkempt sort of warren surrounding a ragged wilderness of garden, which sloped down towards a stagnant pond, sheltered by a clump of trees and usually half-full of dead leaves. And the people who lived there were German Jews, a shopkeeper of some sort, and his wife. The warren and garden, one gathered vaguely, had since surrendered themselves to the railway engineer and the jerry-builder, and a new and more piquant variety of ugliness had taken the place of the old. That was all.

* * * * *

But on one particular Sunday it happened that, for some reason or other, our entertainment was not concluded till later than usual; and the hall where it was held being on the side of the suburb most remote from the station, it was impossible to catch the only train that would take one back to town in time for dinner. I made this vexatious discovery while talking to an intelligent-looking middle-aged man, whom I had noticed sitting in the front seats, and with whom I had once or twice before exchanged a few words, without mastering his name or quality. There was a certain air of distinction about him as if his interests and experiences were rather wider and more varied than those of the ordinary middle-class Londoner.

On this occasion the rector of the place had formally introduced us earlier in the afternoon, and I had learned from him that my acquaintance was Mr. Moultrie, a Queen's messenger, a man deservedly respected, and one of the leading residents of the place.

With Mr. Moultrie, then, I found myself walking away from the hall, with no very definite object, in the direction of the railway. It was a dull, cold November afternoon.

'Your train,' said the Queen's messenger, looking at a heavy gold repeater, 'will be leaving now. By the next, which goes in half an hour, you would have to change.'

We walked on, talking of other matters—music, the opera, foreign cities, and scenery—and I was mentally deciding to go by the slow train, when Mr. Moultrie intervened. 'Could he persuade me to dine quietly with him, and go up by the nine fifteen?' I could not but accept gratefully, with rather a feeling of relief that he had not used the ominous and *banal* expression, 'pot luck.' I should be most happy; but I had to think of the time, I explained.

'Do you live near the station?'

'Two minutes' walk from it,' he answered, 'and on the line. I daresay you noticed——'

I stopped him at once with a question that anticipated his information. He lived, of course, at the house cut in two by the railway, and that house, now known as the Grove Park, was, it appeared, the remains of the manor-house of which I had heard a little, and imagined a good deal more.

All the 'Park' had been covered with rectangular streets of the kind already described. Three-quarters of the garden and a corner of the house had been cut off by the North Midland line; and Mr. Moultrie, the Queen's messenger, had leased the rest of the property at a cheap rental, partly from a curious fancy, partly because it was near the station.

My anxiety to make the intimate acquaintance of a Queen's messenger—a person whom I had always pictured to myself as booted and spurred in quasi-military fashion, and carrying a small valise, ready to post off in any direction at a word from his sovereign—was enhanced by this curious coincidence. And there was a certain independent confidence and cheery smartness about Mr. Moultrie that seemed to me to be quite a professional characteristic. He was in fact, as he told me, perfectly prepared to start for St. Petersburg, Cairo, or Berlin with a couple of hours' notice, though he would probably be given more by telegraph. He had been there and, it seemed, to most other places of interest, and seen everything in them that was worth seeing. Over and above this, he was obviously a man of some taste and culture, well read, in a practical sense, though he assured me he did most of his reading in the train, and never travelled without a select pocket library.

His house was a veritable museum of curiosities, mostly collected during his innumerable peregrinations. Well-selected pictures, mostly of scenes abroad, rare maps, and specimens of foreign art, metal-work, etc., covered the walls that were not hidden by closely packed bookcases, in which again works of travel figured largely.

Quite incidentally he had been present, he

told me, at the assassination of the Czar of Russia. He had also witnessed the making of Germany in the great hall of Versailles, where his 'bowler,' which lay on the floor, had, he told me, been inadvertently kicked by the Crown Prince, the dint of whose august toe had never been obliterated. . . . 'There was the hat,' he said, laughing, 'in a glass case.' He talked on, rehearsing miscellaneous experiences, digressing, at a word or question, to this topic or that, always with a certain racy originality and the ease and charm of a man not anxious to talk but confident of entertaining.

A cheerful fire blazed in the grate, and was reflected by the scores of knick-knacks scattered about the walls and the shelves and side-tables. Mr. Moultrie's quiet early dinner was excellent, and washed down with good wine, but it was nothing to the repast provided by his inexhaustible memory.

It was only after a grand tour of the habitable globe that we reverted to the subject of his present dwelling-place, and its singular situation.

Did the trains keep him awake at night? Oh dear, no; not now. He had long since become accustomed to them. Besides, they regulated his daily existence for him when he was at home. He got up by the 7.50 goods, breakfasted by the Yorkshire express, and knew that the down mail ought always to come by before he got through his soup at dinner. It sometimes made the glasses clink ; and, yes, on second thoughts, he had once been waked by a train in the early morning. That was when the 6.35 ran into a coal train, telescoped three carriages, and killed fifteen people, just under the window. He had run out in his pyjamas and fetched the first doctor to the spot. Lying on the crowded mantelpiece was a large splinter of wood, painted on the smooth side. 'That was thrown on to my roof,' he said. 'In the carriage that it belonged to every soul was killed.' The window ? Yes ; it was at the end of a passage leading to the part of the house which had been removed to make way for the line. Opening a door at one end of the dining-room, he showed me into what seemed a long, narrow closet, hung with many and various overcoats and waterproofs on pegs. At the end was my port-hole ; and underneath it, on a small table, a compass and a species of seismograph, which registered the vibrations—a fancy of his own. You could look through the glass and have a restricted view of the line, but it would not open. The company would not allow him to have a window that opened on to the line; and the wall was very thick, a double wall in fact; and the sleeping rooms were all on the other side of the house.

Mr. Moultrie's knowledge of the neighbourhood was as exact in detail as his knowledge of everything else he had occasion to know. Besides, he was, he boasted, 'the oldest inhabitant,' or nearly so, having been settled in the place just twenty-five years. It was an awful place—yes. But, he added rather illogically, with an accent of kindly reproach, some one must live in the awful places, or it would be worse for those who had to.

For himself, he was not afraid of a dull neighbourhood. Possibly any one else, he admitted, might scarcely care to live in that house.

'Because of the trains?' I suggested. Oh, no; there had been no trains when he first came to the district—at least, the nearest station was two miles away. There was then a stretch of garden and park, if you called it a park, beyond the railway. But outside the park, which was fenced in almost all round by a high wall, half ruined and tumbling down in places, there were already a good many rows of houses and half-made streets, and outside that again the real country.

'Was the old manor-house haunted?'

'Well, no,' said Mr. Moultrie, 'not exactly' —though there were stories when he first came and lived at a house down the road, of a strange beast that walked about the Grove Park shrubbery and shrieked, they said, like a fiend in torment, which was not altogether untrue. But, in fact, the place had been the scene of a dismal tragedy, more dismal than anything in the surroundings past or present. In fact, it was the great legend, the literary tradition, of the place—ancient already by virtue of the modernity of all the cottage-villas in which it was still talked of with bated breath, and overpowering by its sensational horror the respectable, commonplace dulness of their associations. 'There is time to tell you the story from the beginning,' said Mr. Moultrie, looking at his watch. 'I have often thought of writing it down.'

He rose and shut the heavy felt-covered door upon the passage, excluding a good deal of the rattle of a luggage train that banged and blundered by; poked the fire, poured out a couple of glasses of port, pointed me to a long and deep armchair, and drew his own towards the grate.

'Before I came here,' he said, 'a Mr. and Mrs. Sharon Fulksay used to live in this house. That was when it stood in its own grounds, as I told you, in comparative seclusion from the suburb growing up about it.

'The Fulksays—his father was alive then—were, I believe, Hungarian Jews, not Germans, for a wonder. The name should properly be spelt Fulcsai. The old man always represented to my mind that most odious type of low, greedy, and rather prosperous "foreigner in England" who reminds you rather of a pig that's got into a garden. The son was a little more polished and presentable.

'But it was his wife, a good deal younger than he was, who attracted attention and for a few months made such a stir in the place as nothing else ever did or will. At that time it was always, "Have you met young Mrs. Fulksay?"—"Did you see Sharon Fulksay's wife?" For the Fulksays kept a good deal to themselves, but people would turn round and stare at *her* in the street; and no wonder.

'She was a rare beauty—a Creole, I believe, with some Spanish blood in her—a gypsy, you'd have said; just a little of the panther style of beauty: dark red cheeks, and a mane of rough, wavy hair almost the colour of indigo, and worth a mint of money; lips scarlet as a geranium against her brown mouth, and eyes that flashed at you like lightning out of a cloud. Oh yes; I knew the Fulksays—to speak to; and dined with them once, in this very room. They didn't seem to get on very well together then; and I shouldn't have cared to go there often.'

'An instinctive aversion?' I asked.

'Not altogether that,' said Mr. Moultrie with a curious expression. . . . 'She was a bit too lively for him, I thought. It was worth golden guineas to see her when she was angry or amused, and to hear her talk quick in Portuguese and broken English; and she spoke it not like an ordinary foreigner—there was something in her accent that made you want to encore frantically the simplest words she tried to say. To see the girl laugh, you 'd want to kneel down and pray to live with her for evermore; but in one of her tempers—not that it was her fault generally—she was just like a hurt creature glaring round for a spring. She had teeth as white as a squirrel's, small brown hands, and a smart, well-knit figure, like a boy masquerading, but that her feet were too small and pointed. She was active and wonderfully strong for a little woman, and moved about a room, even in the dresses he made her wear (having a Jewish taste for display), like a rope-dancer in tights and spangles, fidgetting to begin. Some said she had been in a circus troupe when quite a child, but I don't believe it. People living an active life in hot countries, where little clothing is worn, often have that air. Whatever they say of her, I believe she was just as good a girl as ever came out of a nunnery. . . . What did they say of her? Why, that he, Sharon Fulksay, bought her as a slave somewhere out in the Brazils. . . . Slavery 's not abolished there? Well, it is in theory, not much more. And I can tell you (what not everybody knows) that in

1875 there were half a dozen respectable London houses owning slaves—some of them hundreds of slaves—in Minas and Bahia, and about there. They might have put you off with some legal quibble, but that 's the fact. Business is business, and you can't always wait to reform a country, least of all South America—though there have been many reforms there, especially on paper—before making money out of it.

'As to that, do you know how the Pygraves of Streatham Lacy made their money?' He mentioned the family name of an eminent millionaire philanthropist—a staunch supporter of Church missions, temperance reform, and other pious causes.

'You don't? and as you wouldn't guess till this time next Sunday, I'll tell you. But I wouldn't repeat it anywhere in public. It was the grandfather of the present Lord Pygrave; a Scotch gardener he was, and he had a partner who was an Irish groom, and they had a small property with a sort of hostel or large shanty upon it, by a port somewhere in the South Seas, where all the slavers—that was in the palmy days of the trade—used to put in for water. And after a bit—I don't know which of them had the idea—but the gospel truth is, that they took to buying up the damaged bits of cargo—the sickly ones, you 'll understand—nursing them up till they were well, and selling them at a large profit—for of course it was a speculative business — to the next comers. Well, the two worked a plantation *afterwards*; but that 's how they made their money to begin with, and plenty of it, I know. You may say, considering what was often done with sick slaves, that it was a philanthropic business. P'r'aps it was, in a way. I don't go in much for philanthropy myself, though I try to be true and just in all my dealings. But I can quite fancy that a man who thought his money had been come by in that fashion wouldn't sleep very easy till a good deal of it had been given away. . . .

'But we were speaking of Mrs. Sharon Fulksay. As to the particular province she came from, San Paulo, I believe, the Belgian Consul wrote a book about it only last year — I have the work on one of those shelves somewhere,—a country stuffed full of poisonous beasts and freaks of nature, you know—serpents, chegoes, talking-birds, pliable stones, plants that eat insects, and insects that turn into plants. Slavery he found in full swing, enforced, as he wrote, "by a whole arsenal of punishments," handcuffs, cat-o'-nine-tails, *tronco de pes*, etc. On the *fazendas* there he more than once saw a veritable "man in an iron mask." . . . It was to prevent them eating earth, a favourite form of suicide! so he says. As to the instruments, and other curiosities of the country, Fulksay, who had been out there once or twice, kept a small collection in a corner of the hall here, where the railway now is. Not in the very best taste, you might think, after his singular marriage; but he wasn't a man of any particular taste, wasn't Sharon Fulksay. And that's not exactly the truth, either; for I always fancied him a fellow who might have had a private *penchant* for slave-driving, if he had had any opportunity for exercising it. There was cruelty, if I'm not much mistaken, and cowardice in the fellow's shifty green eyes and hooked nose—something like Mephistopheles in the opera. But, not to speak of one's own impressions—prejudices, perhaps—and merely to give you the facts of the case, it is a certain fact that before they had been here for three months incredible stories leaked out through the servants of how Mr. Fulksay treated his young and beautiful wife. If the worst of them had been proved home, a bench of bishops might have lynched him with an easy conscience. . . . I'm not boring you with these local traditions?' said the Queen's messenger, while for the fifth or sixth time the floor vibrated steadily to the piston of a passing train. He shifted the lamp-shade, and then poured me out another glass of wine, saying, 'I'll keep an eye on the enemy. . . .

'Well, to go back a bit: their first meeting was by all accounts a curious one. Fulksay himself used to talk about it in early days. He was out there, you see, once a year or so upon some business of his father's firm. They did fairly well once on a time, some sort of produce-brokers in the city; but failed afterwards, and never had a very high character. Then the son set up in a line by himself, something rather shady, if not actual "receiving." High-class R.S.G., as some people whispered. "Dealer in curios and works of art," he called it. Brought in a good deal of money in a quiet way, though for that matter they had a narrow squeak in the law-courts once or twice. But that was later.

'And the last time he was out there, as I was saying, on business, and stayed at some planter's house. In the country it was, and not far from the sea.

'Sharon Fulksay, I should tell you, was a smartish fellow to look at, in his Mephistophelian way—tall and thin, with a rather wolfish smile, prominent teeth, and rather too diminutive hands and feet for a man, suggestive of a certain type of bookmaker or pickpocket. He set up for being quite a lady-killer, however, after his fashion. There's no accounting for tastes, even in experienced women. No man who ever looked him between the eyes would ever have trusted him out of sight with twenty pounds, least of all with a girl they cared for. However, as I say, he was presentable and had money, and so passed for something in those parts, being an Englishman—save the mark!—and the only son, it was said, of a rich London merchant.

'And there he met this girl, so they say, neatly dressed, and stepping quietly about the place. And they fell into conversation—just a few words, nothing more. But he thought her wonderfully affable for such a beauty, and she seemed very pleased to talk to him. And the next day or so they met again—that was before he had been there a week—and he asked her how she liked the country, and how long she meant to stay in those parts.

'And she looked at him just like a servant, you know, waiting for orders, with her little brown hands folded on a white sort of apron she had on over her dress. And while he asked her what she thought of the country and how long she meant to stay, her eyes just opened and sort of flashed at him, and she gave a little surprised laugh; and then she pursed up her lips, and looked at him as it were with a sort of melancholy, but answered quite respectfully, and as if it was no affair of his: "I, senhor? but I am a slave, born on the property." And if ever there was a man "knocked silly," as they say at the music-halls, that man was Sharon Fulksay.

'However, the short and long of it was that he was madly in love—such love as a man like that could know—with the girl. That is to say, he was carried away by her beauty and colour, her eyes and her laugh. And he begged the girl—Santolina was her name, a pretty one, I think—to marry him. And she, it seems, consented as far, she gave him to understand, as her consent could be effective, she being by the law of the place some one else's property.

'And this person, as it chanced—the *fazendeira*, to whom the plantation, or great part of it, belonged—they have large estates out there—was a good and pious old lady who had brought the girl up, and given her a superior education, for a lady's-maid, or sort of companion, which was pretty much her position in the household. Among other things she had to look after the old lady's pets, parrots of every imaginable size and colour, and other birds kept in a great aviary out of doors, as is common in that country.

'Although in the newspapers out there you may see black and white slaves advertised for sale every week—the lighter complexions of course fetch the higher prices—the institution is in practice more domestic and patriarchal than you'd ever believe. But in a case like this the senhora, being advanced in years, felt some anxiety as to what might happen to the girl, Santolina, at her death, when the household with the land would pass, it seemed, to a relative who managed her property and an adjoining estate of his own—a man, however, for whom she had little regard. So the good old lady, being anxious about the girl's future, preferred Fulksay to her heir. If she was right, you will be able to conjecture what sort of a man the latter must have been. He had, however, to be "squared" in some way—a family compromise, I suppose, though he could not actually prevent the diminution of the estate by so valuable an asset. So the upshot of the matter was that Fulksay got the girl (who may have shared her mistress's anxiety as to the future, and certainly felt grateful to him, if nothing more) with her own consent and in part-payment of a commission or some debt which the planter was not quite ready to liquidate in cash. And the two were married, and came home together by the next mail.

'Mrs. Fulksay, I've heard, always had a certain spirit and independence of her own—a bright creature that would have kept many men happy as kings to humour her every fancy, and about as much like Sharon Fulksay (if they could only have seen it) as a humming-bird is like a toad.

'Not but that she did her duty by him, and bore his ill-usage when many a one of her blood would have wanted to knife a man. But they had differences from the first, and even on board the liner that brought them home. And, oddly enough, one of the first trifles they quarrelled about—though they soon found other matter—was a pet bird, a young hawk, that she had brought with her from the plantation. They called it a hawk, but it was more like an eagle in size when I saw it, and a fine-grown bird, well able to fly, but they kept it usually in a strong iron cage. Later, its wings were clipped, and then she sometimes let it out in hot weather for the run of the garden, where it would flutter from tree to tree and come to be fed when she rang a little bell, or called it by name. Fulksay didn't like that bird. He was not a man to care much for animals, even of his own species. And I must own that I never thought it a very attractive pet. Anyhow, he was always saying (which angered his wife) that he would have the beast killed or sent to the menageries at Amsterdam, where, by the way, they would have been glad to have it at a good price; and I think he meant to send it there. For the bird was a fine specimen of the *Tapu-tara*, or Brazilian Fish-Hawk, of which full-grown males have been known to measure five feet across from wing to wing. They call it a fish-hawk, but it is practically omnivorous. In a wild state it kills swans, ducks, rabbits, and other animals. In natural history books you can find it described as a bird of the most singular habits, with a "scream not unlike the laugh of a maniac."

'One of the most peculiar tastes of these uncanny creatures is for catching rabbits by waiting for them at the mouth of the holes. This bird had been known to do that once or twice, for there were rabbit-burrows still left in the park then, on that rise by the fir-trees about a hundred and fifty yards from the house; and they watched it from the windows or the verandah. If it missed the rabbit the thing would dance in the air and peck up the turf—that's a way they have—and throw it about, screaming all the time, so you'd swear it was bewitched by some evil spirit. And one very curious instinct about these birds is that they can't stand the colour of *red*. Some say that it is because the sailors and fishermen on the coast where they live, who climb up after their nests, usually wear red caps and jerseys; others because red is the colour of raw meat and blood, which naturally excites them. Anyhow, if you wanted to irritate the bird and make it scream, as Fulksay did every other day—his greatest pleasure was to be tormenting something—you had only to wave a bit of red rag outside its cage. And once when the servants left out a red cushion on the lawn, they found it in the morning torn to shreds, and a large strip hanging like a flag on the poplar. And it made such a ghastly noise, no wonder that some people were afraid to go by the place at night, or swore that Fulksay had a familiar spirit on the premises. It was a common joke among his city friends that he was so like a certain personage, which was flattery, if "the Prince of Darkness is a gentleman."

'But that bird's "laugh"—you see, people could hear it from outside, passing along the road, and there was only one place where you could see into the garden at all, to make out what the noise came from. And the beast would be mostly out of sight in its cage. Nobody who had heard the noise could forget it. It was just like the clatter of a light stick drawn across railings, but with a ghastly sort of creak at the end. At a quarter of a mile off it would have made you jump out of your chair and run to the window. But the beast only laughed when in the greatest excitement. At other times it simply screamed like a rat in a trap—quite a homely and comfortable sound, by comparison—or "barked" (that was the beginning of the laugh) like an asthmatic terrier.

'In colour it was a dirty grey, with a black crest, and white under the wings; and when it was let out it used to flutter up on to the broken bough of the poplar that still stands on the lawn, and sit there preening its feathers and barking now and then at the passers-by on the road, which was some little way off.'

A wave of thunder seemed to roll quickly by the house, and the red coals shook down in the grate. 'The night mail,' said the Queen's messenger, nodding his head in its direction. 'She's three minutes behind time. Let me give you a cup of coffee. You needn't leave here till ten minutes past nine. . . .

'Well, to go on about the Fulksays. As I said, they kept very much to themselves. Not that there were very many in the place who would naturally have visited with them. Besides, she was too beautiful for the women, and he, it was soon found—in spite of his living in one of the largest houses of the place,—was not quite respectable enough for the men. So after the first stories concerning her got about, they were left pretty much alone. And Fulksay, who was never troubled with any weakness of the heart, soon began to weary of her. At best, it rather seemed she had been a sort of toy to him, a piquant luxury you wouldn't find in England. But whatever he may have once felt, in a few weeks he was running after another girl—a white one this time, with silky flaxen hair. Then she suspected him, and grew jealous—it is bad when such women grow jealous,—and she frightened him once or twice, and that brought out the brute in him. And he swore he would send her back to the Brazils; and she, I dare say, half-believed he could and would do it. For that matter, she might of course have had a separation, but there was no one to tell her that, even if it would have been any use. So she lived on, the life of a prisoner in gaol in a foreign country, without a friend to help her, and fearful, as she said afterwards, that he would kill her some day—unless she killed him first, as she was often tempted to do.

'Not but that, in spite of her saying so, she would, I know, have borne more—far more—on the chance of their living in peace and quietness again, being hot-tempered but not of the revengeful, designing kind. And in spite of what some slanderous tongues hinted about her—you know what a place like this is; such a story would feed them fat for years,—there never was a shred of evidence to show she had a hand, one way or another, in his—his end, which came soon enough. It was more like the finger, not to say the fist, of an indignant Providence; or, as some frankly said, the Evil One come by his own again. Upon my life, it 's hard for a Christian to say what else could be meant by such a scaly horror polluting the quiet respectability of a place for evermore.

* * * * *

'It had been a sweltering day in July 187–.

'The weather was so hot that here in Grove Park the bird I told you about had roosted in the garden the night before. Usually it hopped into its cage in a corner of the verandah at sunset, but with the thermometer over eighty it seemed to prefer the fresh air ; and in the afternoon it had not appeared for its food, and no one knew what had become of it.

'Mrs. Fulksay suspected her husband might have given his long-threatened order for its execution. And Sharon, when he came back from the city and had walked from the station, was in one of his lurid moods. Something large and risky in his "business" had gone wrong, and it was on his nerves.

'He came into the house as usual, wearing a frock-coat buttoned up, and had just put down his silk hat in the hall, when a telegram arrived which did not improve his temper ; and he crumpled it up and threw it on the floor, which was a good thing, for it turned out very useful afterwards at a certain criminal trial. Then he went into the room where his wife was, and they had words almost directly about something trivial. Fulksay cursed because he couldn't find a straw hat, and then he cursed the hat, and then he cursed her for not finding it. And next it seemed—all this came out in the evidence of the servants—they got upon some more serious altercation: some scheme of his, connected with his money difficulties, that he wanted her to play a part in by cajoling some third party—begging for him, in fact!—and she declined.

'But the only shred of a suggestion of evidence against Mrs. Fulksay was, that when he called out to her, in his savage way, from the next room where he was looking for his hat, "*Will* you find me something to put on?" she exclaimed something in her foreign tongue, and then said in a rather curious voice, as if to herself, "I will." Probably she merely spoke to her husband in a tone that showed the temper she was trying to keep under, for just then a servant appeared, in answer to his tug at the bell, which might have been heard all over the garden! . . . I can't imagine any one doubting it. But when he came in again, there was a large red smoking-cap lying on one of the tables which it seemed he hadn't noticed, though he had bought it only a few days before. And when he had picked it up and put it on, he swore at the cap and swore at her again for not telling him it was there. Then, either because he was bent on quarrelling or desperately anxious for her help, they got back to the other, the serious difference. And he tried to frighten her into submission; and she spoke out angrily. Then he tried to explain away something he had let slip—it was about some business or money affair—that had roused her innocent indignation. But she wouldn't listen. And the servants outside heard her voice rise higher, but couldn't tell what she said in her broken English; but from his angry answers, they thought that she, in her turn, threatened to do something, take some step she thought right, unless he gave up his point; and then that he swore she should not have the chance "*till he was out of harm's way.*" And from this and something he let fall about the time, it was inferred that he meant to make a bolt of it that night. But they, the servants, couldn't hear more just then, for the voice came nearer, and in a minute Fulksay went out into the hall, and back into the room again, banging the door behind him. Then there was a violent scene—

worse than any they had known before—and they heard Mrs. Fulksay cry out once. And then Fulksay went out on to the tiled verandah, and the girl inside was very quiet, and at first they half-thought he must have killed her.

* * * * *

'The only witness to what followed was the telegraph-boy who was going back by the path through the shrubbery. And when he heard voices and high words he stopped and hid behind the bushes to see what was the matter, and the first words he heard were Mrs. Fulksay saying, with her foreign accent, "No go out like that, Sharon. Let me . . . me *promise* not . . ." He couldn't make out more, being about forty yards away, and he didn't dare go nearer, for boys were mortally afraid of Fulksay, the "tall, black man." But she spoke, he said, in an earnest, pleading voice, as if "with the fear of death upon her," as it may have been, perhaps, yet not of her own. From inside the room, which had one French window open and one blind down, you could see the garden and the ragged poplar that shows still over the wall of the railway. But the man walked out on to the grass and towards the tree, not looking in the boy's direction (which he was glad of), but turning round to snarl at the girl that he didn't want her promises, and (much what he had said before) that she might write or say what she—pleased, or go where she pleased, when he was out of the way (then he laughed and showed his long teeth), if she could.

'"He wasn't going off himself?" Oh, no; not directly,—if he meant to go at all. It may have been merely his pleasure in tormenting her; one can't say. At the far end of the lawn was a summer-house—I've had it moved nearer the house now—where he used to sit and smoke and take his papers. In fact, they afterwards found a tin box full of them—rather compromising ones—buried under the floor there. He would have destroyed those before leaving, if he meant to leave. Anyhow, he went out of the house smoking and looking more like Mephistopheles than ever.

'I wish I could tell you the whole story as that boy gave it in evidence. I have the printed report somewhere, but can't put my hand on it just now. He was an odd sharp-witted lad, of a degraded literary turn, brought up, like so many of our juvenile criminals in the metropolis, upon revolting "penny dreadfuls,"—which was why some thought at first he had been lying. But it was only the sensational style of his language, which couldn't often find scope for employment in the telegraph business. What he saw in those five minutes of that bright summer afternoon sickened him, I dare say, of all the moonlit monstrosities he'd ever read, and gave him the real horrors for a month afterwards.

'It happened that Hereford Buckmore, our young superintendent of police that was, and a friend of mine, who had just come from a great temperance *fête* at Nutberry Hill, where there was a biggish crowd, was walking home up the new road outside the Grove Park, when the boy, white and scared-looking, ran into his arms. The police have a natural predisposition to stop all persons running anywhere in an agitated manner, so he arrested the boy in a paternal manner by the shoulders.

'"What's up?" said Buckmore.

'"I've seen——" bursts out the boy, and stops for breath.

'"What have you seen?" says the superintendent, sure that something serious *was* up.

'"*I've seen the d—l flying away with Mr. Fulksay.*"

'"Nonsense," said Hereford Buckmore; but he whipped out his tablets. It 's not often a policeman gets a chance of noting down such "information received." And then he made the boy tell him his story from the beginning, which didn't take long.

'It seemed that, after delivering a telegram at the Grove Park, he was coming back through the Fulksays' garden—though he knew that wasn't allowed—because it was shorter, and he wanted to be off to his play; and he had been right into the bushes, where he had no earthly business, after something of the sort boys are always after. And there he had been scared half out of his wits by an enormous owl which glared at him out of a holly-bush and flew away, as if disturbed, towards the house. Then, when he got opposite the windows, came this other excitement—a scene between Mr. and Mrs. Sharon Fulksay. Then, Mr. Fulksay crossed the lawn, and the boy moved a bit to watch him, and he stopped, calling out something to his wife just under the poplar. And just then, before you could wink, there was an unearthly sort of rattle and shriek, and what looked like a great sheaf of thatch fell on his head, right down from the top of the stunted poplar, and "*spread all about him*," and the cigar fell out of his mouth.

'"What do you mean?" Buckmore asked the boy. "What did it look like?"

'And what do you think he said?

'"*Like a tree—a palm-tree in a hurricane.*"

'The boy had probably never seen a palm-tree in his life except in some cheap illustration, but he stuck to his account. Then he saw that the sheaf of thatch on Fulksay's head was something alive—an eagle, or, as he thought, the foul fiend that had got him at last. . . . The wretched man's body, he swore, rocked to and fro: and the long pointed wings of the hawk flapped up and down, to right and left, like a windmill. Then he shook it off once, and it rose and struck him again and again till he seemed dizzy and wild with pain. And then it fastened on his neck, and the man cursed and screamed and cried, and flung his arms about, and the great bird beat its wings on his head and shoulders with the noise of a stick beating a carpet, and laughed and barked all the time like a whole pack of demons in full cry. You see, Fulksay had bullied and teased the beast as he did his wife, and besides he had the red thing on his head which it couldn't bear. Well, he suffered for all his sins—if he didn't repent of them—in that minute; and he gave one wild cry (the boy said it made him feel faint and sick) just as the bird got hold of him. "Help me, Lina!" and she—you see, she had once cared about the man—answered him, so the boy swore, seeming to struggle hard with something behind her—"Shary, I *can't*!" and screamed for help. But the only servant who heard was in hysterics in the back passage, what with the howling of the man and the laughing and barking of the bird. She had her apron stuffed in her ears, and screamed louder than all the rest. And then the two things, that looked like one monster, such as no drunkard ever saw in *delirium tremens*, tottered and struggled along down the rank, weedy lawn—the tall, thin man in his frock-coat still buttoned tight, and the huge bird flapping about (as if it were fastened to a perch it couldn't get away from), and beating his face and eyes so he couldn't see where he was going.

And they stumbled through the rushes and fell into the pond under the trees at the bottom. And there the man clutched hold of the beast, and strangled and drowned it. But it had done for him, you 'll guess. No woman—no man for that matter—would ever look at him again, not if they could help it. And he was mad, stark, staring mad, too—and that was a mercy—by the time he got on his feet and stamped on the bird in the mud. It was a devil, there 's no doubt—and it wouldn't die, but pecked and tore at his feet till the last. And the man, he knelt on its head; and its tail and pinion feathers sort of spurted up in the shallow water like rushes, and that made him madder, and he stamped it all down, and stamped the mud upon it. And then he turned and staggered up the hill, talking to himself very loud and fast, all in his frock-coat still buttoned, and covered all over with blood and the black slime of the pond.

'By the time the boy had seen and heard all that, he wasn't sure whether it was night or day; and the green trees and the blue sky seemed to him somehow to be all the wrong colour, and he turned and ran as I told you, half-believing the bird was alive again and coming after him.

'Now Hereford Buckmore was a smart and handsome young officer who had made a name already by the capture of a desperate gang of coiners—not the man to shirk any unpleasant emergency. So when he had listened to what the boy could tell him, he started off at the double and was at the house in two minutes. He heard loud cries, rang the door-bell, which none answered, and made his way in at the back, without ceremony, just feeling in the tail of his coat for a life-preserver he always carried there. On the floor of the passage he noticed a crumpled piece of pink paper, which he instinctively picked up and put in his pocket.

'And when he opened the door the first thing that met his eyes was the most beautiful woman he had ever seen, standing in the corner of the room in a sort of agonised stupor, with her hands behind her. Her brown cheeks were a pale olive, and her black eyes deeply ringed and full of tears. And she kept her face turned to him with a sort of terrified appeal, looking, he afterwards said, like an Oriental princess in some famous picture, unjustly condemned to death.

'And in that moment, being young and romantic, though a police-officer, he fell madly in love with the girl, once and for ever more. She stood before him so lovely and so miserable that he could have believed her to be a Greek statue, or some warning vision in a dream, not a mere woman of flesh and blood. But before he had time to speak she gave a quick movement, seemed to spring forward with a violent effort, and threw from her something that glittered and fell with a clink on the carpeted floor out of sight.

'The room was in a half-light, with the blinds, all but one, undrawn since noonday. But stepping nearer, he could see a scar on her wrist and a bruise, as from some beast's clutch, on her neck. And he flared up with rage, quite forgetful that he was talking to another man's wife, and cried out, "Who did that?" And she, seeing what he was, and not sure how much he had seen, but inspired by Fulksay with a vague terror of all "minions of the law," answered, quick as thought, "A bad thief, burgleman, *ladron*. He will have steal my money and go kill my husband in the garden." Her hands were tightly clasped together before her when she spoke then, and her black eyes fixed on Buckmore with a sort of forced and childish suspicion that, even at such a moment, almost made him laugh. But she kept it up so well that, but for the gold chain hanging at her waist, Buckmore would have been puzzled, if he had not been primed by the telegraph-messenger. This, he said to himself—for he had never seen her before—was the beautiful Mrs. Fulksay ; and it flashed across him all at once what such a creature must have suffered living in the power of such a man.'

My host's voice was shaking with the poetic energy of his narrative, and I looked at him askance in the firelight and wondered what that might mean ; but he half-caught my eye, and went on in a steadier voice :

'You see, he hadn't the pleasure of Sharon Fulksay's acquaintance. And though, as I say, a superintendent of police with some experience of murder and outrage in the East End, of women and children kicked to death *de gaieté de cœur* by drunken husbands, he was suddenly overpowered by his own innocent ignorance of evil. So he told me afterwards. At the same time he felt such a novel passion for homicide coming over him as he'd never dreamt of before.

'All this had passed in the time it would take you to walk across a room, when a long shadow fell on the verandah outside, and the girl, forgetting everything else in abject terror, fell with her hands on his feet, crying, "Quick, quick; keep him out, he kill me!" and went off in a faint. Buckmore caught her as she fell, and had barely time to throw her on the sofa before Fulksay stood at the window.

'And he wasn't blinded—no, though you'd have thought so—nor hurt, not to die of there and then; but just mad, raving mad, with bits of weed and rushes hanging about his collar, and such a sight as you might never see in a long campaign.

'And when he caught sight of Hereford Buckmore's uniform and cap, he broke out into all kinds of dreadful mad chatter about his business that might have been heard in the roadway outside.

'"If that's a blue with a warrant," he said, pointing at Buckmore with his long, muddy arm, "get out the back way, and take a cab to the Docks. I've got cabins. . . . Who the d—l let him in, I should like to know? . . . Where's the small heavy bag? Bernstein's have got all the plate. . . . Not that one. Drop it in as you cross the bridge . . . and don't wait to try the notes. They're all stopped. . . . I'll strangle Hiram Cohen for this. . . . Not guilty! No, my lord; not accomplices before the fact. I swear it. Father a respectable merchant . . . with a wife, dressed in red. You'll find her at the bottom of the pond: with feathers sticking up. . . . Take away those things. *You killed her, you know it!*" and with a howl like a wolf he rushed upon Buckmore, who was, as I said, only just ready for him.

'It was something outside the common routine of police business, and under ordinary circumstances might not have seemed a romantic or attractive adventure. But there's not the smallest doubt Hereford Buckmore would at that moment have cheerfully faced a whole detachment of criminal lunatics in defence of the woman whose face he had never seen before, and, for all he knew, would never see again. . . .

'Fulksay in his right mind would scarcely have made a fight of it. As it was, the struggle, though brief, was violent, and Buckmore found himself under the table holding the madman down, but considerably out of breath. Then he noticed lying close to hand a pair of spring handcuffs of foreign make. With some difficulty he opened and applied them to the purpose for which they seemed to have been sent by Providence, and thus what remained of the husband's mind and body was secured and removed before his wife came to.

'Fulksay never did. He died in the asylum a fortnight later. But for that he would probably have died in gaol, where his precious partner in rascality and one of their employés were sent. That, or the gallows, would have seemed the most suitable end for Sharon Fulksay, but that the—the bird—"bird or devil," as Poe says—willed otherwise.'

* * * * *

Mr. Moultrie stopped, and slid out his watch. 'In another ten minutes,' he said, 'you ought to be starting, if you don't want——'

'Want!' I interjected loudly enough to drown the roar and rattle of three trains passing at once. 'I want to know what became of *her*—the girl, Santolina, Mrs. Fulksay.'

'Ah,' grunted the Queen's messenger, getting up out of his chair and somewhat petulantly stirring the fire. 'She married—the year after—Hereford Buckmore, as good a fellow as ever breathed. There was some excitement about it, you can imagine—the couple being so young and handsome—and a great crowd at the wedding, though they didn't intend that,—only it got about, and secretly the people would have liked to *fête* him as a sort of hero, and her as the princess he had rescued—so to speak—out of the ogre's castle, which wasn't so very far wrong, though I suppose any man would have done the same. He has a post in Gloucestershire, and she,' said Mr. Moultrie, half to himself and in a tone of inappropriate melancholy—'I believe she's the happiest woman alive. I saw them there only last year. Three fine boys she has, brown-haired like Hereford, but with her foreign colour—I'm godfather, I believe, to one of them, the young Tartar,—and a little gypsy of a girl. Yes; Buckmore married her—as good a fellow, I tell you, as ever breathed. If I hadn't been sure of that,' said the little man, with a rather forced laugh, 'I could have married her myself.'

He busied himself in opening the passage door, and taking down a hat; but I would not let him come further than the front door.

'Yes,' the kindly old bachelor went on; 'three fine boys and a little gypsy of a girl. I saw them. But he wouldn't come here, not to be Chief Commissioner. You can see your way out?' . . .

I plunged alone into the foggy November night. The light of a straggling gas-lamp or two showed me the lie of the curving gravelled path. Avoiding the damp lawn, I could identify at a little distance the ragged poplar, the remains of the shrubbery, the old garden-wall. I felt somehow as if I had lived in the place a dozen years, and was impatient to leave it for ever.

The long lines of lighted parlour windows in each endless 'row' or 'avenue' of cottage-villas seemed to gleam with quite a cheerful homeliness. Above the murky distance towered the railway station, with the attraction of a gaudily illuminated lighthouse. Passing a tract of waste land, as yet unbuilt on and roughly fenced in, I heard the sound of a boy idly drawing a stick across the rails, and restrained an incipient shudder. The Queen's messenger had left me little time to spare.

As I clambered up to the tableland of the platform, the 9.15 thundered in, and a crowd of home-coming passengers covered the small platform. '*Harnsleigh Grove Park,*' '*Harsly Grove Park,*' '*Harns' Gro' Par',*' bellowed a trio of porters, like newsboys crying the latest murder; while one solitary passenger got in, wondering how they could proclaim the familiar words with such indecent publicity.

'THERE have been joys too great to be described in words, there have been griefs upon which I have not dared to dwell; and with these in mind I say, climb if you will, but remember that courage and strength are nought without prudence; that a momentary negligence may destroy the happiness of a lifetime. Do nothing in haste; look well to each step; and from the beginning think what may be the end.'

So writes Mr. Edward Whymper, in his immortal classic recording the great tragedy of the Matterhorn.

If it is ever easy to forget the latter of his maxims, it is particularly so in the course of a difficult rock climb. There is this remarkable difference—one may remind the reader—between snow and rock: that progress over the former is more or less continuous, while over the latter it is broken, detached, composed (so to speak) of very different, if small, stages. It is this peculiar interest, lucidity, and variety that makes rock-climbing such a delirious joy. Ascending or passing over snow, even when the process is so dangerous that your guide forbids you to speak—and speaking is most often an unprofitable waste of the climber's breath,—is not quite like this. The difference between the first step and the last is, perhaps, only marked by a greater or less degree of excitement and exhaustion.

On the rock, at the first step, you may be in a position which you could hold against two or three men, and from which you could pull up half a dozen if they wanted help. In the next, four or five feet upwards or round a corner, you may very likely be just able to preserve your equilibrium, while the slightest touch—so you feel—would certainly send you over. It is curious how on these occasions that dull dogma, the law of gravitation, seems to take a sort of spirit form and walk beside you. 'One mistake,' whispers this true Spirit of the Alps, 'one undecided or foolish step, and you are mine; no longer a defiant, self-confident human animal—a mere helpless atom, obeying the laws of that dull, dead matter into which it is the next moment to be resolved!'

Imagination and metaphor apart, however, the fact is that when the ground is so difficult that no one of your party is likely to have, so to speak, any superfluous safety to distribute among his friends, there is not much use in being roped.

That is why Leonard Galveston, his friend Currell, and the guide who accompanied them, Hans Weirother, from Samaden, had already discarded the rope by the time they had done about three-quarters of the ascent of Piz Coltella in the Engadine.

The Piz Coltella—a singular curve and pointed spur give the peak this suggestive name—is a rock mountain, one on which scarce a patch of snow lies in summer-time, something under 12,000 feet in height; 'an interesting peak,' connoisseurs confide to you carelessly over the large-scale map and a glass of port, 'if you go up the right way.' Currell and Galveston—Leo, his friends called him—were going up the right way. The friends of the latter (Currell was an older hand), and certain of his female relatives, would probably have thought otherwise. Galveston—a fresh-coloured, keen, athletic young Briton as ever demanded a cold bath in a foreign hotel—was only filled with a wild and pure delight as he and his companions, after a comfortable breakfast, strolled up the winding zigzags of the great Surlej pass. The road is a triumph of Swiss engineering, down which, every evening, the Diligence is to be seen apparently precipitating itself—the collars dancing about the horses' ears—upon the expectant village below.

One of the charms of rock-climbing is that —there being nothing to melt but the adipose tissues of the climber himself—it can usually be done by daylight, without the necessity of poking one's way out of inhabited regions by the aid of a primitive dark lantern.

And the particular peaks to which we here refer have been so constructed by a thoughtful Providence as to give the competent pedestrian a good day 'on the top of the rocks,' and yet enable him to be back in comfortable time to recount his adventures at early dinner.

Which, by the way, is no small part of the attraction attending the many climbs which it is more pure pleasure to *have done* than to *do*.

Climbers, however, professedly seek the romantic something which from the days of Livy to those of Mr. Whymper has mysteriously united pain and pleasure.

Thus Galveston's companions were sedately ready, and he himself was frantically eager for the fray.

There was, as has been said, no cause for hurry. They had the whole day before them, and the sun was not yet oppressively hot.

The Piz Coltella is, speaking generally, a four hours' 'expedition.' That is to say, that if you know the way, or have an eye for rocks and no one else to think about, you can race up it satisfactorily in three and an odd twenty minutes or so.

'We shall be on the top,' said Galveston to himself, looking at his watch, 'by about one o'clock.'

The red spur of the Coltella, visible from the lower curves of the highroad, passed out of sight as the party rounded the last turn and reached the level top of the pass.

There they left the smooth and dusty road, stepped briskly across the green 'Alps,' stumbling over one or two rude stone walls, and were on the steeper grass slopes.

Here the mountain, withdrawing all view of its higher beauties of rocky spine and jagged *arête*, presented a bare, uninviting shoulder of that brown, sun-baked grass which is to the novice, from the treacherous familiarity of its appearance, more dangerous than many a snow-slope.

But half an hour of that vigorous 'scrabbling,' for which one hesitates as yet to substitute the actual comfortable infantine crawl, brings one on to the longed-for rock which, after streaking the turf here and there, as the incline becomes more perpendicular, finally shakes off the scanty clothing and assumes its proper form.

Then you begin to see where you are.

Galveston saw, and warmed at the sight.

Before them stretched upward a long and dreary gorge, filled and choked to overflowing with a chaotic avalanche of dark-red boulders,

> 'confusedly hurled,
> The fragments of an earlier world'—

each about the size of a grand pianoforte.

That was the way up.

Let not the reader suppose the unit of size —a 'grand,' not a 'cottage' piano—arbitrarily selected.

He who has travelled the road will know how important are the exact proportions of the said boulders; how infinitely the difficulty of striding, stretching, or jumping from one to the other, and the corresponding facility of straining your ankle and barking your shins, would be diminished were the obstacles a cubic yard or two larger or smaller.

It is one of those places which abundantly demonstrate the use of a light, stiff alpenstock; something between the 'painted walking-stick' which rouses the contempt and loathing of the superior-minded Alpist, and that variety of punt-pole on the middle of which, as some guide-books say, you should be able to sit. But a climber spends little of his time sitting on an alpenstock, and a great deal, more especially upon rock, in stretching tentatively after the unsurveyed and unknown.

And as to supports, people who need them do wisely to keep off mountains; the chief use of Alpine 'clubs' being to keep the player in easy contact with nature and geology, and in particular to tell him how far he is out of 'the perpendicular.'

To traverse the wilderness just described is,

of course, merely heating. You may break your head, your knees, or even your neck with little trouble at every other step, but you cannot climb.

After forty minutes of this, Leo Galveston looked rather ruefully at his new boots. They were excellent boots, but their novelty had been scarified away for ever. No matter. He shook himself together with a deep delight, and prepared for action by buckling the belt of his jacket another hole tighter.

His whole body was glowing with the deep internal heat wrought only by that violent exercise in which every smallest muscle has enough to occupy it.

Then the party paused for a moment to breathe and look about. Above them towered a great arm of the mountain, like the ruined wall of some Titan's castle built to defy the gods of heaven. The sun glared roundly down upon them as they prepared to scale the silent celestial fastness, lit up the glowing red surface of the rock, and traced with clearly pencilled purple shadows every irregular ledge, crevice, and crack that lined it like courses in its ancient masonry.

Galveston, to whom this kind of prospect was rapture, mutely wondered at the stolidity of the guide, who seemed absolutely unaffected either by the familiar scenery or the coming ascent.

‘The rope here, Herr Currell,’ was all he said, and proceeded to uncoil it.

And up they went, duly roped; Hans Weirother first, Leo in the middle, and Currell last, stealing carefully along the zigzagged cracks, ledges, and narrow terraces here and there lined with strips of thin grass, and lightly feeling their way against the towering wall of rock on the left or on the right.

It was all clean, sound going, perfectly straightforward if you were only careful. After all, a ledge or bracket on which you could not safely stand an inkpot or a drawing-room candlestick is quite enough, and more than enough, for the human foot if put down in a workmanlike manner. And the way here was often as wide as an ordinary country foot-path or plank-bridge, though, of course, there were corners where two out of the three ensconced themselves tightly, and held the third close to the angle of the wall.

Hans Weirother looked round once or twice at the young man behind him, and seemed reassured.

All Galveston's faculties were engrossed by the exercise, but he was going steadily, quite steadily.

There was a moment of embarrassment a little later as they wound their way to a point which gave the first clear view of the higher curves of the arête above them, a sweeping fringe of spearlike jags and fantastic pinnacles which is itself, when you get on to it, the highway up to the summit of the Piz.

Both turned to gaze up the sharp, serrated spine or hog's-back which hid from them the three peaks that mark the top of the mountain.

'This way, Herren,' grunted the guide.

Currell admits that he thought at first Weirother had made a mistake. That way?

The man was asking them to walk across a face of bare rock some thirty feet wide, falling sheer down almost to a picturesque little water-shoot floored with smooth pebbles that was visible far below them—it was the wilderness of huge boulders they had taken near an hour to cross —and Weirother himself seemed to hesitate a moment.

But Currell promptly realised that he was only engaged in untying the rope. The others followed his example.

Whilst he coiled it on his back, Galveston looked at the place somewhat askance.

But what a wondrous thing is faith, more especially in respect of mountains! A peasant or a rustic sportsman tells you with nonchalant gravity to do something that looks—only looks—very like flying, and you proceed to do it, and feel the better and wiser for having done it.

The *mauvais pas* in this case was not so bad as many, and perfectly safe for the able-bodied who believe it to be so—a mere afternoon lounge of the chamois, whose spoor Weirother noted here and there. It is a respectable axiom that wherever a chamois can stand a man can, though it must never be forgotten in applying this theory that the former animal can jump with a freedom and precision quite unknown to the latter.

Of course there was plenty of foothold, if not quite of the horizontal order—a few inches, that is, now and then. You may have to feel for it, but there is no hurry, and a ledge above affords a substantial support from which to swing, if you like, during the process.

'Follow me,' said the guide; 'grip the rock tight and plant the feet firmly. There is no danger.'

'Danger' in the mouth of a Swiss guide is a mathematically ascertained quantity, of which he admits no loose definitions.

'As a matter of fact,' thought Galveston to himself, after they had passed, 'if it were only six feet from the ground—if there were not that lucid and impressive view of the valley below—nobody would think anything of it,' which perhaps only showed that the excitement and the altitude were beginning to tell upon him.

Time being still well in hand, and the haven of the arête only a quarter of an hour or so distant, the three subsided for a moment's rest, each at his own anchorage—a hand or a foot tight against the rock, the eye surveying the geography of the Engadine valley. The smallest loose stone dislodged by a touch fled lightly down to the abyss, skipping hundreds of feet at a time. There was an exhilarating, intoxicating sensation of being in the sky; as the remains of solid earth dwindled to this narrow, pinnacled rampart about which they crawled and clung. An hour more and that would be below their feet. Not very high above them a lämmergeyer floated—a black patch against the pure sky—its shadow, a fainter patch, spotting the rock below. The sunlight bathed them like a flood. The heat was intense, but it was the heat of that dry and vivifying air to which our foggy climate is as a green duck-pond to a rapid salmon-river.

* * * * *

Progress becoming easier for a moment, one of the party turned a little one way and one the other.

A halt was only allowable long enough to admit of these indescribable sensations sinking into the system. Then they pursued their cat-like clamber.

It was still, of course, hard climbing, but trusting to a natural agility which had served him well enough so far, and seemed indeed to be all that was wanting, Galveston, under the impression that he had detected a 'short cut,' and unobserved for the moment by the two others, had turned in a slightly different direction. They thought that he was just overtaking them. He thought to catch them up by a way of his own, and then pass to the right along a ledge some thirty feet above him.

That was all.

He had slung his alpenstock on to the belt of his Norfolk jacket, and was working his way, every muscle strained to clutch now the roots of a grass tuft and now a small ridge of rock. Another ten seconds passed—in this sort of progress it is easy to get hurried—and then a cold fear seized him, like the clutch of some wild beast.

He could not keep foot or hand-hold a moment longer. Could he have gone back? Impossible, or so it seemed. He made a furious effort forward, upward. The wall of rock seemed to project right over him, to force him outwards. Through the only hollow before him he struggled frantically. A tuft of grass gave way, but as it fell he had grasped another. The rock edge at his left seemed to be coming through his hand. One more struggle upward, and yet another. A large splinter of rock, his last foothold, fell rattling down; and he stood erect, breathless and streaming with perspiration.

For one half-second, as his exhausted lungs filled and his strained half-cramped muscles relaxed, did Galveston smile the smile of the victor over a physical obstacle ; the next he turned deadly pale, for he and those watching him saw that his last energetic movement had been a false step, and that he was caught in a trap.

All had passed in little more than a minute. Hans Weirother, carefully placing his heavy ironshod alpenstock in a crack in the rocks, and shifting the bag of provisions from his back, merely observed (but Currell felt that no expression of horror could have been more significant), '*Wait.* The young gentleman has gone too much to the left.'

Galveston looked up again, to be sure that his first glance had not deceived him.

No! The place might have been a niche for a statue—was so in fact—and he, the statue, standing with his face to the wall, with just room to stand, unable to stir three inches to right or left. What was above, around him, he knew well enough, though he could not see now—a blank unscaleable rampart. No one could help him. In front was a ledge—a sort of incision—inside the niche, on to which he held with one hand.

There was no danger of falling ; not yet. He could rest his hand upon the rough face of rock immediately before him, almost touching his body in fact, but that the projecting roof of the alcove made it necessary for Leo, who was a tall well-grown youth, to stoop slightly. The position was uncomfortable, and might be exhausting in time.

Above his head the broken strata of rock shot abruptly outwards in sharp chisel-like ledges. Stretching one hand back he could feel their hard and uncompromising outlines, could thrust his hand into dusky cracks between their splintered edges. No more could he do without over-balancing, and the mere *feel* of the rock, which he could not see, assured him that, without wings, no mortal could rise from his present position.

The view below, on the other hand, though uninviting, was perfectly unobstructed.

Looking between his legs he saw, some thousand feet below him, the dreary chaos of boulders which strewed the mountain's foot. A stone, displaced by his feet, bounded down the precipice. He could hear it, for more than a quarter of a minute, striking the rocks as it fell. . . . Then, as he fidgeted again, a heavier fragment rushed down with, as it seemed, a frantic rapidity; and the noise, Leo fancied, roused him from a sort of stupor which eclipsed the hurried events of his ascent. He appeared to have been standing where he was, dozing for hours in a sort of feverish dream. Then he awoke, with a cry, to a sense of time and imminent danger, and heard the familiar voices of his companions answering him in the strained tones of suppressed alarm. . . .

Five, ten, fifteen minutes passed; yet the voices, beyond vague suggestions of endurance, preserved a maddening silence. Galveston could not avoid seeing what that meant. There was absolutely no hope; and yet *it*, the obvious alternative, remained incredible. How should he be doomed to death, to physical destruction, for nothing? What had he done in any way proportional to this awful and astounding result? The great *prima facie* feeling of its outrageous improbability rushed upon his mind—all the faculties of which seemed working like a mill-race. People did not, nowadays, generally die in this way.

Of course such dreadful things were possible; he had read of them—of the sort of Minos tribute of youth paid season after season to 'the strong terrible mountains.' But no relatives or friends whom he could think of had ever been killed—any more than he was going to be killed—by a headlong fall from a precipice. Surely some warning, some unusual phenomenon, must accompany an occurrence so contrary to all calculation. Its very rarity seemed to constitute a sort of insurance. . . .

And then all the unconscious joy of youth came upon him like a flood, in full photographic detail; his own life with its ever more fascinating struggles and increasing pleasures—the more satisfying conception of it he had somehow arrived at lately; the way certain people, whose favour meant success, were beginning to appreciate what he felt to be his best work—his home, his sisters, his . . .

The idea of giving up the sweets of this existence now, and for what?

The tragical absurdity of being there struck him like a blow. He could have laughed at it. *Que Diable allait-il faire dans cette galère?* Why did he come? Why was he not in an armchair in his own room at home? . . . And then he prayed with furious energy to be saved from the natural consequences of his own act.

Yet he remembered dimly having had a discussion with Currell, the Sunday before, on the grass in front of the hotel, about the theory of prayer, and having thought the latter's views rather antiquated. Views—the most advanced views—were at a hopeless discount now. In fact he was praying as hard—if that can be said—as he had ever rowed in a boat.

Such is the consistency of human nature. Looking down again he saw the valley quietly reposing.

The distant tinkle of cow-bells caught his ear.

Everything else—the whole world—was all right. How idle to suppose its vast serenity would be broken through by any providential interference in his favour. Such miracles belonged but to the region of romance. And yet, and yet. . . .

A voice interrupts his reverie. ‘Move not, move not; all will be well, dear sir, wait only.’ It is Weirother who speaks, in German, the tongue which Galveston has come naturally to associate with all the joys and excitements of mountaineering. There is a note of confidence in the gruff guttural accents of the guide which his actual state of mind hardly justifies. For twenty mortal minutes has he been struggling with a frantic, albeit deliberate, energy of hand, foot and eye, to get near, from one side or the other, or most of all to get above the fatal niche.

It is, as he sees clearly, has indeed seen from the first, absolutely out of the question.

The proper route up this side of the Coltella —the track that brings you on to the arête— lies straight away to the right. All to the left, except in so far as Galveston's present position proved the contrary, was absolutely inaccessible.

Yet Weirother continues to stare fixedly, it would seem, at the boy's head. 'What do I see?' he exclaimed at last. 'Have a care, dear sir; but look. In front, above you, it gives there a ledge and a crevice?'

Galveston reaches back with a trembling effort.

'*Ach! thou dear God! do not try to climb.* It is worse above. I have it tried. Steady then, dearest sir. Feel only—with one hand.

Is it deep? Can you put your hands, your stick, into it?'

Galveston shifts his alpenstock out of the way, and tries with one hand.

'Yes—for about a foot—a deepish crack.'

'So; good. Your knife, Herr Currell, and find me a small stone, I beg. So; good again. Tie it to the rope.'

Hans Weirother is not only the most reliable of guides in the Engadiner Thal, but also the 'Hirt' of the district, most cunning of chamois hunters, and man of strange and various experiences. Currell, therefore, quietly attaches a suitable slip of rock to the white manilla rope.

'Good; throw it over his shoulder.'

From where they are standing, some thirty feet below and a little to one side, this was a matter requiring some skill and care. Currell had bowled for his county, but he declares that he never gave so much thought to the delivery of any missile in his life as when, having carefully cleared the rope, he endeavoured to pitch that rock into Galveston's niche.

The first time it struck too high by about two inches, and rebounded clear of the boy's head, the second it passed in straight as a die, and the trembling Galveston clutched it against his shoulder. As it was, the exciting effort almost overbalanced him, and Currell's emphatic admonition, 'Easy does it, old man,' seemed to fall with an unusual accent upon an unheeding ear.

The most robust animal courage is not proof against every novel and startling variety of terror, or—what is sometimes more trying—the reaction from it. To Currell's eye the boy was clearly losing his nerve. The mere moral effort of self-control necessary to resist the last inviting advances of destruction in such a crisis seem to engross all the consciousness of the victim. 'Stand steady, Leo,' he repeated. 'What will they say of me?—(and in a lower tone). Think of Helen.'

Now Helen was Currell's youngest sister, and her name had not been mentioned in the whole course of the expedition. Nevertheless Galveston seems to recover himself, and takes the end of the rope in one hand. There is a momentary pause. . . . 'Pull it up, dear sir,' mutters the German, 'without hurry'; and Galveston pulls, mutely wondering what will come. At the end is a piece of stout wood shod with iron, some two feet of Weirother's alpenstock, which he has just cut off. 'Can you fix it in the ledge? Firmly—have a care. It is done. Thanks be to merciful God! It will not slip—no? Try it for one eye-wink. Ah! lift only one foot. Excellent.'

Galveston now sees in a flash what is meant, but calmly obeys the orders which follow, passes the rope round his own body, knotting it securely, and then round the wooden pivot; then holding the other end tight, with two turns round his wrist, proceeds to let himself down, slowly down.

* * * * *

'I have done it *once* before, Herren,' explains Weirother, apologetically, 'with a heavy buck chamois, when I could not have carried him myself. See, sirs, it happened upon this wise. I take good aim. I fire. The beast makes an immense leap, and he fell upon a place of that same nature, and lay dead. I climb ten minutes, dear sir, for to reach him. But, *mein Gott*, we must descend separately. Ah! it is bad there to the left. This way. Have a care, sir. It was lucky, very lucky.'

* * * * *

The guide's emotion, or whatever he had shown, vanished even before Galveston had attempted to express his; and the three descended by the other side of the shoulder and reached their hotel almost in silence. As they separated outside the house — Weirother on his way to the kitchen, they to their rooms —the former merely remarked 'To-morrow, Herren, at the same time?' To minds engaged in bottling-up a good deal of strong and varied feeling, the apathy of the remark was almost comic.

'To-morrow.' Galveston could not help reflecting that but a short while ago 'to-morrow" had seemed centuries distant—round a corner, so to speak, of Fate and Time. Perhaps at the instant neither of them felt that they had got quite a secure enough grasp of the present to begin tempting Providence by stretching into futurity.

But after all it was not verbose sympathy that had brought them back to the living, chattering group of tourists and friends in the *Salon de lecture.*

So they contrived to master their emotion,

like heroines of romance, with an effort, while dressing for dinner.

*   *   *   *   *

'Galveston was in a nasty place this afternoon; it was half an hour before we could get him out,' says Currell at *table d'hôte*, struggling to persuade himself that this is a natural and practical introduction to his account of the exploit.

There follows a chorus of the praises of Weirother.

'Whatever induces people to go into such places I never could imagine!' exclaims an interested lady auditor. But one young lady sat with downcast and almost tearful eyes. Leo explains to her meekly that he has no intention of going there again.

'All's well that ends well,' observes the Reverend Hatchleigh Coolwore, M.A., a former President of the Alpine Club, who, during a fortnight or so in August, rules our table at the Schwingli-Horn with a rod of iron, and whose little dog has been up half the peaks in the Oberland. 'But these young fellows' —the veteran drops his voice to whisper in the ear of his next neighbour, an elderly Q.C.;

we only catch the words—'The old story—you remember young ——, rejoicing in his might—, that day on the "Nonne"?—started glissading on the lower slopes—stumbled once, twice—laughed—no danger—head first—all over in two minutes—before their eyes—could do *nothing*.

'Or Jimmie Farlow on the Schlacht-Horn?'

The divine answered with an expressive convulsion of head and shoulders. 'That was a black year for us.' For the Club, he means, and that larger worshipful corporation of climbers within and without it, whose interests and sympathies are one. 'The fact is,' and the seeming platitude is announced just loud enough to reach the general ear, 'in the Alps you have to think about everything the minute before it happens, and not the minute after. That's all. By the way, do you play whist?'

FROM THE DARK PAST

THERE is a pastime or pursuit which to many a Londoner, leading by compulsion a sedentary life, comes to take the place of the sports of the field.

It is, one need hardly say, the sport of book-hunting, which, though usually devoid of danger, provides a good deal of the excitement roused by the pursuit of animated game. It was this common interest which brought me into contact with the vicar (as he has since become) of St. Alboin's, East Kensington, an ardent and mystic ritualist, but a really well-meaning little man, who would, you felt, do anything he thought was right, whatever absurdity it might involve.

Certainly one would never have suspected him of a sensational experience, and when I got upon the spoor of it, I think it did give him a carnal pleasure to satisfy my curiosity.

*   *   *   *   *

I collect books, he began. As curate of a

parish in Bloomsbury, with the remains of what was at the University a taste for reading, this naturally became a great interest in my life. My collection, I need hardly say, is chiefly theological. The Bishop once called in his carriage on purpose to see my copy of Wyclif's *Little Gate* (the English Nuremberg edition, 8vo., 1546), and I have other rarities.

John Lavering (he is a barrister and my cousin, with whom I share our set of rooms) is also something of a bibliophile, but in a different way. He sometimes complains of the amount of space on our shelves taken up by Reuchlin's grand collection of the Early Fathers. But we contrive to live and let live; I even keep an eye open for his pagan interests.

North London, as a rule, is a dull hunting-ground. But one Saturday evening, in the course of a flying round between 6 and 7 P.M., I happened, in a dark shelf of a dirty little shop in a dirty little street off the Euston Road, upon what I instantly saw to be a book of some rarity and character. It was a quarto, bound in the toughest of oak and pigskin, on the sides of which were coloured arms and a coronet.

The bookseller remarked, as I fumbled at the stiff clasps, that the volume had hardly ever been opened, and had only recently been sold out of the library of some French or Italian monastery, where it had lain for some three and a half centuries; all of which seemed very possible. It was entitled in a style not unfamiliar to my eyes, *Elixir Vitæ, sive de arte plusquam divinâ nunquam moriendi Opus Aureum*, etc., etc., and the preface contained an extraordinary collection of passages out of the Old Testament, supposed to bear upon the possibility of prolonging the human existence for an indefinite time. The book was printed, I thought, in Venice, and though it bore no date, was clearly not much later than the beginning of the sixteenth century.

The interest belonging to an old book, I need not tell you, is an interest quite by itself, something which is not in the date, the shape, the size, the printing, the subject, nor even in the accidental memorials of other possessors long dead, but is somehow compounded of all these, though independent of any one of them?

You would know that sort of animal attraction like the appearance of a likely cover to a keen foxhunter, or the look of a secluded untried pool to an expert fisherman ; the feeling of having one's hand upon some mysterious, perhaps long-lost thread of humanity, going back to the dark depths of the past ?

Such feelings are sometimes delusive ; in this case they were not. The memory of the book, which I have long since destroyed, is a very monument of horror. But this is to anticipate an experience far remote from my imagination at the time.

I confess to a lurking interest in what bibliographers call occult literature, in which one sometimes stumbles on strange forecasts of modern thought and research, half-learning, half-charlatanry.

What puzzled me about this book was the colour of the paper, a curious pale green. Paper indeed fades to all kinds of colour, but not paper of this date, nor paper which has hardly ever been exposed to the outer air, as was obviously the case with this. For that matter, early specimens of the printing of the fifteenth century are often found in a similar condition. Perhaps, it suddenly struck me, this might be a copy printed on specially coloured paper for the use of some distinguished personage. This, in so early a volume, would render it a historical curiosity. Could I have made a mistake as to the date? A second glance at the title-page reassured me. Between the lines of print an early and picturesque hand had added, in Italian, after the first words, a line of manuscript signifying that the volume (or something contained in it?) was *returned with very many thanks to her most illustrious, pious, and learned ladyship the Duchess of Ferrara by her most sincere, humble and devoted slave Cola of Sinibaldo.* The first words, *ritornato con moltissime grazie*, were clearly enough written; the rest of the inscription was faint; the date at the end very clear, *a* 22 *di Maggio.* 1506, *di Ferrara.*

The whole seemed to have been indited in a hurry. There were light scratches of the pen visible under the words 'most pious and learned (*dottissima*)' and across the printed word *vitæ*

Clearly, then, the book had been printed before the end of May 1506; so, having paid first the sum of seven and sixpence, I determined to take it home and let Lavering, who was something of an Italian scholar, revel in the deciphering of the mysterious inscription. I may mention that more than one interesting discovery has fallen to my lot from the study of the early manuscript one finds in or about old books.

Once, indeed, we unearthed the better half of a letter, reflecting severely on the motives of Martin Luther, in the back of a Hebrew Testament printed by Bomberg in 1529. Lavering has a wonderful nose for scenting out these things. For all which reasons, having carefully tucked in a loose fly-leaf, I was in the act of putting the volume under my arm, the sniffing middle-aged shopman having retired to his innermost apartment to procure me change for half a sovereign; when a voice from the darkest corner of the shop suddenly addressed me by my name. The voice, and its tone of mysterious earnestness, recalled me abruptly to the outer nineteenth-century world.

Not knowing that there was any living being in the room but myself and a disreputable-looking cat, which lay asleep on a pile of dingy folios, I started and dropped the book, which fell open again, upon the counter.

The voice was that of a girl whose appearance, now that I observed her leaning forward with her head in her hands on the far end of the counter, which was almost hidden from me by a huge edifice of dusty calf and vellum, was quite familiar to me. Looking at her now, it struck me at once that she must be the daughter of the proprietor, who, as she made out the bills of the establishment, would naturally be acquainted with the name of so frequent a customer as myself.

There was then nothing so odd in that as there was in her hurried accent of suppressed anxiety. When I turned she quickly advanced, slunk towards me, I should say, until we stood opposite one another with only the barrier of worn and blackened mahogany between us, beneath the flaring gas-jet. I could see she was a handsome girl, but untidily dressed, almost dishevelled in appearance, and very pale, not an uncommon feature in London girls of the working class. Before I could say a word she went on in the same tone: 'You'll see Mr. Rainsleigh, sir, won't you, to-night or to-morrow?'

Rainsleigh, I should tell you, was a medical

student with whom I had recently had occasion to come in contact, but not the slightest wish to be further connected. Young, not bad-looking, brought up in vulgar opulence by a self-made and misguided father, I could never make out why the fellow had ever been put to the medical, or indeed to any particular profession. The only result so far had been that, before he had been a couple of years in town, he had attained the reputation of a decidedly 'fast' man among his associates at 'Bart's.' I confess frankly to have no prejudice in favour of medical students. It may be that they represent a sacrifice demanded from humanity to their noble profession. Its very studies, perhaps directly on account of their tremendous actuality, seem to have on the whole a rather crushing and coarsening effect upon all those not endowed with unusual strength of character and diversity of intellectual interests. Rainsleigh, however, had, as the common saying goes, never had a chance; and I inclined to regard him, if one can so speak of a mere boy, as a hopeless young reprobate, in whom a vulgar badness bred in the bone had duly manifested itself in the flesh.

I now remembered that I had observed him in the shop once or twice with some surprise at his presence amid such surroundings, and that we had exchanged words there only a day or two before. Not wishing for a moment to be regarded as Mr. Rainsleigh's friend, yet anxious to help the girl if I could, I answered somewhat vaguely, 'Well, I don't know that—you see—I might perhaps, but——'

'Then you tell him,' she interrupted with fierce energy, but speaking low and putting her face close to mine, 'on your faith as a clergyman, that if he doesn't—hush!—I'll write it. Father won't let me get out, and you'll take it to him?' The beauty of her anxious pleading face moved me, so that before she withdrew it I had half unconsciously let slip the promise she asked for.

Our singular colloquy, broken off by the reappearance of my bookseller with two shillings and sixpence, had not lasted more than a minute. The girl quickly and silently snatched up from the counter before me a square sheet of paper (I did not notice at the time how it came to be there) and rustled back to her former place in the half-lighted corner, while the old gentleman apologised for his trifling delay. As another customer, entering the next moment, distracted his attention by one of those enigmas which occupy so much of the attention of second-hand dealers, and I turned to leave, not forgetting my precious volume, I felt that the girl slipped into my unoccupied hand a note, and also that it was written on something rougher than ordinary note-paper.

The next moment I was in the street, wondering, in some vexation, of what sort of an ultimatum (for of its desperate character I could not doubt) I had suddenly become the bearer. A little more presence of mind would doubtless have enabled me to reject the singular commission altogether.

I am not sure. It is, of course, not for us to assume that we are in any seemingly trivial conjunction made instruments of Providence, still less of Divine Judgment. Yet, when I consider how the mere accident of my visiting that particular shop on that particular evening of all the year involved me personally in a sort of responsibility for the most dreadful event known to my experience, I confess I can with difficulty shake off the idea of an all-pervading design, in the execution of which we poor human agents drop unconsciously into our places, but of the actual working of which it is only allowed us here and there to catch a dim mysterious glimpse.

The night was cold and foggy, and coming out of that stuffy gas-lit room, after the ten or fifteen minutes spent in the examination and purchase of my latest 'find,' I pulled my overcoat about me and stepped out along the greasy pavement, streaked with its thousand dreary reflections, in the direction of home. Rainsleigh's lodgings, it was true, lay almost directly upon my way, but I was as yet undecided whether to take the note there myself or to send it by a servant. Circumstances settled the matter for me.

The bachelor home of this gilded youth was in Great Buildford Street, and as I paused in hesitation at the corner of that old-fashioned thoroughfare my ear caught the sound, not altogether unusual in those parts, of voices (one of which I seemed to recognise) engaged in noisy and trivial altercation as of gentlemen who 'have been dining.'

I was right enough. It was Rainsleigh

and his fellow-lodger, one Flackstow, whose association with him I had never been quite able to understand, even on the ground that the possession of money covers a multitude of failings.

On the other hand, in return for whatever indirect benefits Flackstow may have derived, he had, I knew, done his best in a hopeless endeavour to reclaim the young prodigal, as indeed his present conduct tended to show. Neither he nor Rainsleigh had, as a fact, dined, but the latter had been playing billiards and incidentally drinking a good deal. Not drunk, but flushed and excited to a degree which exhibited his natural self with a painful publicity, he was at this moment enlarging to Flackstow upon the beauties of a certain music-hall dancer, upon whom apparently one of his recent companions had been casting reflections.

Flackstow's part in the discussion dealt not so much with the disputed qualities of the young lady as with the question how far it was necessary to proclaim them to all the passers by. In other words, he was evidently anxious to get Rainsleigh quietly home and prevent his making an exhibition of himself, and the two had hardly reached their door when I overtook them. 'Can I come in?' I said to Flackstow, feeling that the moment was not one I should have chosen for the visit. 'Come in?—oh yes,' responded Rainsleigh with noisy familiarity. 'The more the merrier, and' (reverting to the subject of discussion) 'I'll show you her photograph—and see what *he* thinks, eh?' and he turned to Flackstow with a grin which was not reciprocated.

We passed up the carved staircase of one of these fine old panelled houses which recall the departed glories of dingy Bloomsbury.

Rainsleigh's long sitting-room was furnished with that sort of sumptuous barbarism which moves despair as much of civilisation as of morals. The art of inferior sport and the *demi-monde*, with the most worthless literature, encumbered an apartment which looked all the dirtier for the richness of its ill-kept furniture. The chimney-piece was garnished with coloured photographs of eminent actresses; a pack of cards lay scattered over the table and the floor beneath it. In one corner of the room stood an open piano littered with the most worthless and revolting types of music-hall song; and on the large mahogany sideboard stood a bottle of champagne and several tumblers. The atmosphere had a dull permanent flavour of stale tobacco.

Among these uncongenial surroundings I endured a minute or two of hesitation and embarrassment, wondering to myself why I had come into the house, why I had not delivered my commission in the street and gone straight home.

I have said I knew nothing of the fellow, beyond what was involved in meeting him on one or two inevitable occasions. And though I judge no one, and should not, I trust, shrink from contact with any human being for a good end, perhaps I might wisely have avoided it in the present case. To decide exactly how far by not doing so I made myself responsible for the dreadful event which followed is a matter beyond human judgment, though it cost me many a sleepless night.

I am aware that I had a strong prejudice against Rainsleigh. In fact my sympathies were already so far enlisted on the side of the girl, with whose affections I now conceived him to be playing in a characteristically heartless manner, that I had determined to give him the note myself. If he asked me any question about her, I would then answer it in a manner which could leave him in no doubt as to what an impartial person must think of his conduct. It may be said I was jumping to conclusions, and that his supposed conduct did not concern me, unless from an accidental ambassador I chose to become a partisan. As to that, I must confess that I was partly moved by curiosity as to what he would say.

Flackstow, as if with an inkling that I had paid my unusual visit for some purpose possibly more or less connected with the 'cure of souls,' had meanwhile turned up the gas, and merely observing to both of us, 'I 'm off—due at the hospital,' flung out of the room and left me to execute my embarrassing mission.

'Oh, Rainsleigh,' I said gravely, 'I was asked to give you this.'

With a quick glance of surprise he took the note from me, unfolded and read it through. The document was not, as indeed I knew it could hardly be, one of many words. What those words were I never knew, but of their effect there could be no doubt. His whole face flushed with a violent emotion, compounded, it seemed, of wrath and shame not unmingled with a certain fear. It was this excitement (I can only suppose) which prompted him to address me in language which, combining an uneasy and impertinent air of suspicion with one of still more unpalatable confidence, gradually drew me into a conversation of the most undesired and unexpected kind.

I had not retreated at the very instant of fulfilling my mission, simply to avoid the appearance of timidly evading a natural inquiry; and having become so far involved I hardly know what enabled me to go through the trying scene that followed. But the conviction grew upon me that, putting aside all conventional relations between man and man, here was an opportunity offered me, at the cost doubtless of some personal suffering, for arousing in this objectionable, if not abandoned, youth some glimmerings of a latent moral sense.

It was a mistaken impulse.

To my surprise I found him, encased in his glassy conceit, descanting to me glibly, and as he thought persuasively, upon what he considered his own superior merits in regard to the female sex, and to the one victim of his charms in particular. It was the strangest experience.

Dropping into a chair opposite him and laying my book on the table I watched his face, which indeed to the believer in physiognomy offered little encouragement. The shallow forehead and coarse animal lips did little to redeem the babyish, if once handsome countenance, in which a stupid affectation of sneering self-confidence strove to displace its native inanity. Taking my amazed silence for an evidence of sympathy, perhaps admiration, this swaggering Don Juan of the Students' Quarter continued for my benefit his volatile discourse.

I had better have left the room before hearing these confessions, since they provoked an inevitable altercation which soon became a passionate diatribe on my part.

I do not know what I said to Rainsleigh. At such moments, even with the best motives, one says and does many things which sound grotesque enough when recounted afterwards in cold blood. That I abused him roundly and fiercely, and that this at first caused him some surprise, I remember well enough. I strode about the room ; I stood over the fellow —with no fear of his anger, for I could see that he was a coward ; I sat down again. I tried to talk to him gravely and quietly, watching his face all the time, and praying that I might detect there some trace of compunction, or at least of embarrassment. Turning round once in the middle of the room I noticed him fidgeting uneasily with the letter I had brought. Again I wondered what sort of desperate message it contained, and whether a coincidence between its language and my own might not be working in him some change of spirit. Then an insufferable reflection of his upon 'Life'—in the 'Tom and Jerry' sense of the word—set me off again. 'Life,' I cried, 'what do you and such as you know of Life? *Are you fit to live?*' . . . Did some such question momentarily cross his own mind? With an absent air of awkward distraction he slowly tore the paper of the girl's note into strips, as if the mechanical exercise relieved his feelings. I strove to reason with him. 'A helpless human being,' I urged, 'might forgive him. She might be incapable of revenge ; but there was, after all, a judge to be reckoned with. The mills of God grind slowly, but——' Was he listening? He seemed at that moment to hear only the sound of my words, and sat there crumpling the scraps of paper into pellets, which he half unconsciously (or animated, as I fancied, with a desire to destroy all traces of the letter) thrust into his mouth and chewed viciously as if chewing the cud of bitter and remorseful thoughts.

So I imagined, and it is possible the young reprobate passed through a momentary struggle (the whole scene lasted but a few minutes) with himself, or what remained of conscience in him. But when I ventured in my ignorant misappreciation of his feelings to touch his shoulder, he shook me off with a rude and angry gesture, and all the coarse violence which stood the youth in place of manhood came back to him. . . .

I am glad that it has not often been my lot to listen to such language, which, however, fell upon my ears, as I beat a dignified retreat, with no more effect than, I fear, my exhortations had produced upon his spiritual sense. I remember his calling down the staircase, in hoarse accents of condensed irony, a pressing invitation to have a drink, 'as I must be [to translate his execrative adverbs] extremely thirsty.'

Vastly relieved at the conclusion of an acutely painful experience, in forcing myself to undergo which I could only hope against hope that I had acted for the best, I hurried homewards. Having forgotten that it was one of my night-school evenings, on which my fellow-lodger and I share an early nondescript meal, I found awaiting me a half-cold repast and many reproaches for my abominable unpunctuality. The latter emanated, of course, from Lavering, as he lay, fed, slippered and velveteen-coated, at full length on the sofa, with a pipe in his mouth and an auction catalogue in his hand. He was silenced, however, by the short account I gave him, between mouthfuls, of the scene with Rainsleigh. I finished my dinner, and had been peacefully smoking with my feet on the fender for some twenty minutes, when my companion, having reached that stage in the evening when he walks about the room like a restless polar bear, picked up the *Elixir Vitæ* from a table by the door. 'Hullo! what's this?' he ejaculated, subsiding at once into a deep arm-chair with the volume in his hands and his back to the lamp.

'Oh,' I said, 'I want to ask you about that manuscript note on the title-page. Who was Cola Sinibaldo?'

He looked up from a careful examination of the binding. 'Cola Sinibaldo!' was his reply; 'then you 've been reading my Bembo's letters.'

'No, I haven't,' said I, taking up off the sofa a heavily gilt and beautifully printed little book, the *Lettere del Cardinal Bembo*, published by Comin da Trino in 1564. As I laid it down, taking care not to remove Lavering's marker, I noticed that it was the third volume of four, and contained letters addressed *to Princesses and Ladies*. 'No, I haven't; you 'll find his name written on the fly-leaf.'

'The fly-leaf's gone,' interpolated Lavering quickly. I then remembered where and how it must have slipped out of the book. 'No,—I 'm going to sleep,' I added; 'I mean on the title-page, of course.'

There was a pause, and then an exclamation from the arm-chair, 'Great Scot! if that isn't extraordinary!'

'Well, tell us all about it,' I said. 'Who was Sinibaldo, and who was the Duchess of Ferrara?'

'Cola Sinibaldo? Why, I was reading a letter to him only an hour ago, a letter from that immaculate divine at your elbow. I say, I should have thought that this book had never been opened since it was bound, except by him—Sinibaldo I mean, not the Cardinal—when he wrote this; and I wonder why he crossed out the word *Vitæ*, and why he underlined those complimentary adjectives *piissima* and *dottissima;* some very obscure joke there, eh?'

'One thing at a time,' I expostulated. 'You were quite right; it has hardly ever been opened.'

'Wrong,' he pursued, with the tone of an expert; 'I think you'll find you're wrong. It's been messed about, scribbled upon, and some rascally bookseller has tried to clean it with beastly acid that comes out of the pages now—bah! I must go and wash my hands,' and he rose to leave the room, shortly reappearing with a towel.

'Who were they?' I persisted.

'It's astonishing!' he replied irrelevantly.

To get anything out of John Lavering when he is interested you have always to proceed by indirect inquiry. 'Was he a friend of the Duchess's?'

He laughed aloud with startling vehemence. 'Not much,' he rejoined, sobering down at once. 'The fact is he knew rather too much about her antecedents and her family relations, which were not exactly suited for publication. You can make it all out from two or three of these precious letters. You see, she——'

'Who *was* she?' I repeated.

'—She made three or four unsuccessful attempts to get him out of the way. He had got hold of two or three very dark secrets, and began to find the air of Ferrara rather unhealthy.'

'Yes; but my good fellow——'

'Oh, I'm coming to that in a minute. It was a very near thing once or twice, but he was a smart man, and something of a chemist too, so whenever——'

At that moment the man from the ground floor lounged in and distracted Lavering's attention for a minute or two. Before he was gone, the night-school in Blue Lion Square demanded my attention, and I did not get there till late.

It had not struck ten the next morning, and Lavering, who had been breakfasting with his friend downstairs, had not yet come up, when Flackstow with a pale face slid into our room, and shutting the door behind him, leaned towards me, keeping hold still of the handle, with the breathless exclamation, 'Will you come round? *Rainsleigh is dead!*'

'*Dead?* Impossible! What do you mean? How did he die?'

'Poison of some sort. And that's the strange thing. Browser, our analyst, doesn't know what it is. The girl Sankey, daughter of that little bookseller you know, is suspected. They have arrested her. It looks bad; she seems to have sent it him in a note. They think she must have had it by her a long time.' Here he let go the handle and came towards me holding out something. 'It seems to have been wrapped up in this paper. He had a piece of it crumpled up in his hand when—when we found him.'

I spread out the scrap of paper on the table, but as I did so my hands trembled and I shrank back with horror.

'Be careful,' he stuttered, 'there is poison on it still. I must keep it for the inquest.'

'On this paper?' I said. 'Do you know it is four hundred years old?'

Flackstow stared glassily, as at a madman. 'How do you know?'

'Know!' I answered. 'It is part of a blank leaf out of this old book,' and I held up the *Elixir Vitæ*.

At that moment I heard the voice of John Lavering as he came up the stairs, whistling in a leisurely manner an air I had often heard him whistle before, though I don't fancy he has ever whistled it since—*Il segreto per esser felice.* He swung into the room, and stopped dead at the sight of our two horror-stricken faces.

'Lavering,' I cried, and caught him by the arm, mine trembling the while with a ghastly excitement. 'Lavering, about that book!'

'I looked at it again,' he said, 'and I believe you and your bookseller are right after all. It *has* hardly ever been opened, and never read, or cleaned, or anything. Yes, I have looked it out in Gamba. He says it was probably printed at Ferrara early in 1506; and this must be very rare, as only a few copies were produced in quarto for the Ducal Court. That explains everything. The pages stick together; the old mediæval trick, you know. I dare say it was lucky I washed my hands; and, by the way, I advise you to put it in the fire before it does any mischief. *She* put that mixture on for the benefit of Sinibaldo. The inscription is his answer to her present, the Elixir of—don't you see—*Death*. But what's the matter with you?'

'One word more,' I said, still holding him. 'You have not explained yet—what I asked you last night—*who was Duchess of Ferrara in May* 1506?'

'Who was she?' he blurted out,—'the Duchess of Ferrara? Why, man, didn't I tell you?—*Lucrezia Borgia*.'

MY FIRST 'KILL'

It was in Switzerland, and at the above mentioned Schwingli-Horn Hotel that I first met old Ffalby Ollyatt of Ollyatt Shaws. Though an athletic-looking man and sunburnt—every one is sunburnt in Switzerland—one would never have taken him for a country gentleman. There was a flavour of old-fashioned leisurely culture and 'letters' about his conversation at dinner; and he set Hatchleigh Coolwore right about a quotation from Persius. In fact we all took him to be that commonest of educated impostors, the disguised college-don. That was, however, before he got into the smoking-room, where over a wood-fire, as the conversation passed from mountaineering to other sports, he told us this veracious legend of his youth.

* * * * *

We shall never know in this world what it was that frightened that mare.

Who shall explain the doings of the equine race? Their sensibilities are an unmapped area;

their foolishness an unfathomable abyss. I myself, *moi qui vous parle*, have known a horse of several years' unblemished character fall asleep in the sun, slip a foreleg on cobble-stones, and recovering the same, bolt hysterically, as if overpowered by the mere discovery that it possessed the usual complement of limbs.

The very mare I speak of, ay, and a first-class made hunter she was, with the shoulder of Behemoth, as you might have said had you seen her storming up one of our heavy ploughs of a stiff, sloppy, autumn afternoon with fourteen stone on her back—my dear old father never rode less, and he was in the saddle only a fortnight before he died. That very mare, I say, has stood with me, times out of mind, with her head over the parapet of the smaller railway bridge, and snuffed the smoke of an engine that passed panting and shrieking underneath her, as if she thoroughly enjoyed it. Perhaps she did. Perhaps she had reason in the other case too. Having all the love of a Pheidippides for her and her kind, *equini nihil a me alienum puto*.

But to get back to the beginnings—of myself, as it must be in this case—and of this story. Though come of a riding stock on the male side, and with an inherited passion for the saddle, I was by nature a delicate and nervous child, one result of which—that I was educated at home by a private tutor, without spending the best years of my life in laboriously learning not to learn at a public school, as did, by their own confession, so many of my contemporaries —I have never altogether regretted.

As eldest son of the house, I was the subject of a good deal of anxiety. 'It is his heart, doctor,' my poor dear mother used to say, 'that gives us so much uneasiness. I could never bear to——'

'The heart,' broke in our wiry old provincial Galen—I can see him sitting there in his old, brown, strapped riding-trousers—'the heart, madam—I beg your ladyship's pardon a thousand times—the heart wants exercise as much as any other part of the body.'

To this original but not abstrusely scientific argument (which struck my mother a good deal) I owed, I believe, my first pony. From this to an occasional mount on one or other of my father's hunters was a natural promotion. It is a singular fact, which some will verify from their individual experience, that I deliberately underwent quite indescribable torments—spiritual, not bodily—in the process.

In truth I was keen enough. A passion for the stables, for horseflesh, for the kind of glamour that pervades the dullest country when viewed from the heaving back of the animal which the old Greeks thought 'the glory of proud luxurious wealth,' possessed me from childhood. At fourteen I am sure I had all the literature of sport's golden age, Surtees, and 'Nimrod,' at my fingers' ends. Assheton Smith and Dick Christian had no secrets from me. All the theory of seat, hands, and venery that could be learnt from books I knew. Nothing, in fact, interfered with my learning to ride but an unfortunate want of 'nerve,' which kindly coachmen and respectfully reticent grooms hinted behind my back to at least one disappointed parent.

Well, some of us are born brave, some achieve bravery, and some have it thrust upon them. This latter case, or something like it, was mine on the eventful day when Boadicea bolted with me down the High Street of Fryers-Ashby, and created an incident in county history which is still a precious tradition among the shop-door gossips of the place, and will in another century of conservative iteration develop belike into as splendid a myth as any enshrined in Homer.

Before that time let me record the 'historic germ' of an episode which, however it may tell or read now, was a five-act tragedy condensed at the time.

To those acquainted with our old-fashioned market-town of Fryers-Ashby, the expression 'High Street' will present no idea of superabundant stateliness or space. These were only exhibited, if at all, in the market-square before the old Guildhall, with its stained Jacobean windows, finely carved gable-ends, and pilastered basement, which resounded on every wet Tuesday to the lowing of many flocks and herds. The town itself, respectable for its historic flavour and well-preserved 'stocks,' was a picturesque congeries of narrow and crooked streets rudely floored with cobble-stones, and darkened by the beetling brows of many a homely old black and white dwelling-house. And on its outskirts, here and there interspersed with tracts of high, well-coped, and moss-grown wall, showed some half-dozen of those long comfortable fronts of the type every Englishman loves, the genuine 'well-gardened,' 'country-town' homestead.

I saw little of these beauties that dismal November morning when our oldest stableman drove me into Fryers-Ashby by an unusually circuitous route—for the 'High Street' was 'up,' and in fact all over the place, the result of a recent sanitary scare—on an early visit—of all cheerful destinations!—to the local dentist.

It was, in truth, for all the mild drizzle, fine enough for hunting purposes—one of those dull, undelusive forenoons that ripen into a good 'working' day; but the Fletchley, then our nearest pack, was not out; in fact, my father, on some municipal business intent, was to ride over on Boadicea about twelve, and drive home, to give me the pleasure of an hour on the mare's back before luncheon, a meal which for a variety of reasons never took place at all.

This—the ride that is—was, even as a reward for the martyrdom of dentistry, more than I deserved, having but two days before, in the presence of my father, who was trying a new hack, disgraced myself and annoyed both him and the mare by openly 'pulling' the latter at a small fence which she could have cleared standing.

Nevertheless, it was a moment of deep and unalloyed delight when, followed by the elderly 'Zeb,' whose deep mistrust of my riding capacities induced him to follow me, with the horse-rug on his arm, out of the stable-yard of the old 'Falcon' Inn, where so many a blown hunter has been refreshed by a pail of 'half and half,' I rode out into the aforesaid market-place, booted and spurred, and, truth to tell, with a lurking sense of not being 'the real thing,' but a fraudulent imitation thereof.

The jingling bell in the Guildhall turret was clanging out the hour of noon as I turned the mare's head homewards.

It was at that very instant, when I had scarcely had time to settle myself in the saddle, sort the reins according to my methodic fashion, and pull down the curb, that *it* happened.

The place was full of groups of farmers and market-women, loafing rustics, and street boys. A flock of sheep were passing close by. Some say it was the sheep-dog (an ill-bred lurching brute, I remember); some, a stick thrown at him by his owner; some, with more probability, a stone missile aimed by one boy at another, that bounded from the roadway, and struck Boadicea sharply on the withers, or a foreleg. So much for conjecture. The fact is that she threw up her head, spun round like a teetotum, and before I knew anything had disturbed her mind, was off in a wild scared gallop across the open space before us, with the said sheep-dog and two or three other curs shrieking at her heels as if to complete the rout.

The ancient Zebulon was the first to see what had happened. The old man tore along the pavement, but for a few yards, as he never ran before or since. Then, catching his feet in the horse-rug, he fell, with a sprained ankle, in the gutter, yelling to me, 'Sit down and ride 'er or you're——' A frantic chorus of alarmed and excited bystanders drowned the rest of his admonition.

That all this happened in the market-square was a drawback in one way, since it allowed the mare to get up steam, for at the first shout and the sound of horse-hoofs on the stones, the scattered groups parted to right and left, leaving us a practicable 'corso,' but for a few misguided sheep which went down before us, the contact with their awkward bodies driving Boadicea yet wilder with fright. On the other hand, it gave me something like a hold of her before reaching our first fence. I have said that she bolted in the direction of the High Street, and that the High Street was 'up.' Citizens of any properly managed English municipality will know what that means. It was a chaos of obstructions. Locomotion of the slowest was barely possible to a careful individual. Locomotion at a rapid rate to man and horse was obvious death and destruction in something less than a minute. That the whole scene could not last much longer than that—nor so long as the reader will take to peruse this page—was tolerably certain. Nor did it.

The 'first fence' was more than a fence; it was, at least to my terrified glance, a substantial barricade; in fact, a good-sized beam erected on crossed posts, and covered with sacking, was stretched across the roadway, flanked with a few loose paving-stones, odd baulks of timber, and workmen's tools and clothes. Nothing very formidable, you may say, but for the chaos and night beyond it. . . . I had never yet gone at the simplest jump without 'craning.' But the sudden intensity of this real danger so far drove into my senses the recumbent groom's advice that I believe I rode all that I knew.

As to holding the mare, I had no time even to think of trying it. Had the obstacle been a brick wall, or a plate-glass shop front, she would, in her insensate panic, have gone headlong into it. As it was merely a low piece of timber, she simply flew it, from instinct, grazing the cross-posts and scattering minor objects to left and right. As we landed in the watery clay of the roadway I saw what was before me.

In bad dreams I sometimes see the place still. Immediately in front of us was a deep drain cut across the street, with a stack of four-inch pipes ready to be laid ; on the farther side, ten yards beyond, was the open waggon that had brought them, drawn up as if to barricade the passage, and flanked with more paving-stones, and beyond that I knew there was bound to be another barrier like that we had just got over.

That was all one had time to see, as the scared navvies fled like Russian gunners before the Light Brigade. Two, however, were at work in the drain, and a score of bystanders, with the fatuity usually exhibited on such occasions, shrieked at them to 'get out.' A more sensible ganger on the spot simply bade them 'lie low and look alive,' which they accordingly did, making the best defence possible with pickaxes against the shower of pipes sent crashing down on them from the heels of Boadicea. It was as awkward a leap as possible, just at a curve of the street, and as she landed, all anyhow, in deep mud, among the rubbish beyond, and close to the narrow pavement, I made sure the end was come. But it wasn't, and though you could just feel her head, there was no stopping her. The obstacles she touched flew this way or that like things bewitched and of no weight; and just when I made sure of her rolling on me with a broken back, she came round a point or two with a fearful effort, sent a shower of cobble-stones into the nearest windows, reared up and tore wildly ahead, straight for—that at which few of us have ever found it necessary to ride—a long waggon some five feet high and half-full of iron piping. In the couple of strides allowed us her gallop had steadied. It was no longer a mere blind rush. I was well down in the saddle, and had some hold of her. By the most frantic of efforts I might perhaps have pulled her to one side enough to risk the passage between the ends of this formidable barricade, the slippery pavement, and the wall. But — great heavens !—at what a risk, even if there had been no danger beyond. Men conversant with riding accidents know what self-preservative virtue lies in keeping straight, and how much the simpler forms of destruction (where safety seems past praying for) are to be preferred to the more complicated.

But of the whole frenzied escapade this was the most blankly terrifying moment. Inaction, vacillation, would simply be death quick as the fall of a guillotine.

I need hardly say that by this time the whole street was alive, every door and window flew wide, and every tongue clamoured excited suggestions and interested expressions of alarm. The 'assistance' of so large and noisy an audience, while it did nothing to allay the terrors of Boadicea, may perhaps, so powerful is the sympathy of humanity, have done something for her rider.

I jammed my heels into the mare and drove her at the barricade in front of us with a wild confidence that she would go through or over that or anything.

One vastly exaggerates the effort involved in a horse's jump. A friend of mine was in Piccadilly Circus the other day when a four-in-hand bolted. One of the leaders (a well-bred hunter) jumped, without encouragement or hesitation, at a four-wheeled cab, and fell, in fact, right across the driver's knees. But for the harness and an unsympathetic companion, it would undoubtedly have cleared the whole vehicle.

There is nothing, therefore, very surprising in the fact that Boadicea, dropping her haunches like a deer, rose straight at that waggon and alighted inside it. It was the first pause in her wild career, and though it lasted no more than twenty seconds, can only be described as agonising. A horse, one knows, can stand quite comfortably with all four feet on the top of a beer-barrel; but one unexercised in that kind of gymnastics will find it difficult to balance itself on a pile of pipes rolling backwards and forwards in a cart. It was at this moment that an elderly sporting butcher, who had known both myself and the mare from infancy, called out emphatically from his shop-door to a man on the other side of the street, 'Now stop her, you ——' (the imprecation, though personal in form, merely expressed the trying seriousness of the situation); but the individual addressed, reflecting probably that it was one thing to stop a horse, and another thing to escalade one dancing in a cart and threatening every moment to jump upon him, did nothing. The butcher threw in a second barrel of counsel. 'Throw a sack over that far rail and she'll jump it too.' A prompt individual on the spot at once carried out this timely suggestion. The 'rail' referred to was a bit of rope or iron wire stretched from iron rods erected in the roadway and shutting off the traffic on this farther side, a nasty obstacle which many a horse would fail to see. I knew nothing of this, I need hardly say, till afterwards—'Could I get the mare to stand for one second,' was my only thought, 'in this maddening situation, or to jump down?'

But Boadicea, feeling her foothold going among foreign bodies of an embarrassing nature, did what every animal of spirit would under the circumstances; she 'let out' in one wild explosion, kicking half of the side of the cart through several plate-glass windows. Breathless from this frantic effort, she had barely time to fall on all fours and find her balance before we were touching the last barrier sideways on (I tried to pull her straight, but there was no time). Sideways on she took it, off all feet at once, and I heard the ring of one of the iron stanchions as a hind hoof sent it spinning on to the pavement; and then, and then all was over, but for a fearful corner to turn—a thing that might well have been fatal alone at the pace we were still going. Lord! how I hauled at her reins, for opposite us was a blank eight-foot stone wall, and the cobble-stones had a deadly slime on them from the morning's drizzle.

Twice she bowed her head and shoulders, and the flame flashed from under her feet to right and left as they 'scrabbled,' like a terrier at a fresh-run rabbit-hole, on the slippery kennel. Twice the crowd yelled out, 'She's down!' and the second time a hand almost reached her bridle. But by that instant we had turned the angle, and Boadicea, recovering herself, more terrified than ever by the experiences condensed into the past minute, and by the efforts of the crowd, sprang forward again with the bit between her teeth, and shook off the precincts of Fryers-Ashby at racing speed.

The dangers of being run away with in open country are not very appalling to the experienced horseman. It would have seemed incredible to me at that moment that but a few months before I had fallen off my pony from sheer fright (coupled with a slight uncertainty as to stirrups) at the pace he was going.

Boadicea was bolting now at a far more alarming rate, but my only feeling was one of triumphant excitement. Yet it was no small relief, as the sound country road gave under her flying feet, that the scared flight—after some mile and a quarter of fair going—subsided to a strenuous and determined gallop, and that as we breasted a sharp rise I felt her straining head answer to the helm.

It was at this point, just before the turn down under the trees by Copleston Spinney, that the mare pricked up her ears, and mine caught a new sound, that which no shire-bred man, woman, or child has heard for a century gone without some stirring of the blood. At first the soft intermittent tinkle as of cups or glasses on a board, then the broken chain and ringing cadence of distinct metallic notes, last the full volleying chorus of two score of fox-hounds, howling in full cry.

With no more thought of following the road, I steadied Boadicea at the gate facing us, and with a snort of impatience she sailed over into the deep plough beyond. The hill was steep, and we cantered and slithered down it, holding her hard by the head, and both in the very crisis of suspended excitement, for from the crest of it, as we rounded the spinney, both of us saw and heard the pack—a waving streak of white—heading straight away up the grass vale.

By the time we were down on the level, and after one breathing canter, the whole field were far ahead. One could see the black and red dots of a trailing second flight as they rose and fell automatically, like the dampers in a piano, over the farthest line of fences.

Then came our hour of triumph.

Who shall rush in, where so many masters have trod, to describe the transports of a 'good run'?

But to have that run, a 'run of the season,' nay, of many seasons, for one's first! To be well mounted, and a feather-weight; to feel the world, or the finest grass country therein, before one; to choose one's own line, with the supreme new-born rapture of feeling that one can ride it! Oh, respected critics and readers, in this ever more sedentary world, is not that something?

To be fast as wax in the saddle, warm set to a reeking, untired steed, whose neck is still 'clothed with thunder'; to have melted off, as it were, in the very fever of motion all feeling of 'mounted' humanity, and attained the intoxicating, bird-like, boat-like sense of floating and tossing 'across country'; to catch the light, petulant 'worry' of the snaffle-bar as you draw in the long neck, as one draws a strong bow, in time for each straight, arrow-like stride of a mighty hunter going fresh and strong under you!

Thoroughly distracted from her late alarms,

Boadicea snuffed the battle from afar, and shook herself together, as she danced over the first low hedges and rattled her heels in mere skittishness on the stiff top of a clean white railing, for the familiar race. There was no hurry.

Field by field and fence by fence did we overhaul those flying forms of red and black.

For full five minutes I remember (and there is a wild joy in this kind of companionship) going flank by flank to a farmer-looking fellow on a tall, lashing young chestnut. It must have been for a mile, even by mortal measurement, that our two horses strode like clockwork together. Together they quickened, reared, rose, fell, and steadied again, as brown quickset or yellow timber straightened across our course. And when, lolling back in the saddle, we dropped at a more leisurely pace into the long pasture below Yappingham Manor, it was the mere joy of 'going' that inspired me to call out, 'Whose hounds are these?'

'Lard Sudbery's,' ejaculated my friend, without turning his head. And then, having made his line for the silver streak rapidly broadening into view—the sort of brook at which you can hardly go too fast—jerked out with a stiff shake of the snaffle: 'Rin to airth by Ashby . . . secon' fox.'

Now Fryers-Ashby was on the very outside of Lord Sudborough's country. It was clear they had found their second fox about mid-day, and were running home—home, that is, from their point of view; but from mine, and the precious mare's, the very opposite. I finished that reflection as Boadicea, swallowing all the rein I could give her, spun headlong at the sixteen feet of water, and landed a yard on the other side without dropping a step. An ejaculation of approval was jerked out of the man on the chestnut as he slipped across lower down with such precision as to send half a hundredweight of turf into the water, and, stroking down the excitement of his inexperienced mount, drew a little to the rear.

It is a fact that the bliss of that long afternoon was once or twice clouded—for a second or two, shall we say?—by the reflection that we, for the mare could not be blameless in the matter, ought to have gone home. The difficulty—if I recollect rightly my subsequent explanation of it—lay in determining the precise point at which it became an imperative moral duty to pull up.

For, as the news spread of our astonishing adventures in the streets, it need hardly be observed that my father, informed that we had last been seen performing circus tricks in a railway van, had at once taken the nearest horse, and with other equestrians who volunteered the pursuit, ridden, as he hoped, to my assistance. On getting out into the country, they were much surprised to see nothing of us.

I, on the contrary, should have been extremely surprised to see them, or any other living thing of which the mare, in her then frame of mind, had had three-quarters of a mile start. And she fairly astonished me. That 'second fox' had kept us going, with scarce time to draw breath or tighten a girth, for over twenty minutes (during most of which time I had been racing for a place), yet this was but the overture of his performance.

The hounds were now half a mile ahead, and the 'ruck' of the field, most of whom had had some good exercise in the morning, had almost tailed off as we splashed through the stiff water-meadows of Little Yappingham, and toiled across the tiring 'ridge and furrow' above the mill.

In the country we were here skirting, this eternal feature of its conformation, so desperately trying even if you take it diagonally, is repeated in large by a regular and killing succession of long, small, but steep hills and deep valleys calculated to break the back of most mortal steeds. Five or six of these tiring climbs, garnished with a moderate amount of fencing, five or six of these descents, cantering and slithering over the grass slopes—I holding the mare's head hard till we sighted the small ditch or bush-covered streamlet that regular as clockwork divided the fall from the rise—and the wildly superfluous energy of Boadicea seemed for the moment to have evaporated.

She was still going strong under me, but steady, except for an occasional rush at the ditches, at that pace which is the crowning virtue of a made hunter, when 'the going is all done for you,' and the rider need only think of his or her line, and the hand of a girl dropping 'light as a snowflake' on the snaffle is enough to condense the quickening gallop into the steadiest of leaps. Thus Boadicea. A glance to right and left showed her an object of envy to heavier weights than myself.

Many of our select company had sought a smoother, if more circuitous, route on the highway, where the sound of fast trotting, and the sight of more than one pink coat and velvet cap bobbing above the hedge marked the line they were taking. The military-looking man on the black, whom we had been half-consciously following for the last two miles, subsided for the moment, seemingly 'all to pieces,' into a particularly soft corner at the bottom of the last hill; a regular customer, in a brass-buttoned vestment stained to Tyrian purple, rolled over, just clearing his horse, at the next slippery rise. I remember opening a gate at the top for a little lady on a grey thorough-bred, half-stewed but game as ever.

From the brow of the long ridge of pasture we saw against the dull and misty November sky a grey-blue line of gables, topped by a tall and pointed spire, fringing the horizon.

'Thanks. Do you know where we are, by any chance?' said she of the Arab (a countess of the bluest blood,—but all bloods, human and animal, are heated to a like temper on such occasions as these), leaning down to pat her favourite's reeking flank.

I could not inform her ladyship; but the customer in purple had followed us through the gate at the far corner, leading his mount, a sturdy-looking chestnut that snorted like a grampus. The rider's coat was more draggled than before, and his breeches and the very ribs of his hunter were plaistered with yellow mud. Looking up from his occupation of mopping the miry animal with a handful of rough grass, to doff a battered hat in our direction, he panted—

'How do, Lady Cranstoun. Grand run, eh? This ain't one of our foxes.'

He swung himself into the saddle again, and stood up in the stirrups.

'One of the Archdeacon's bagmen, p'raps; . . . . and, by Jove, he's headin' straight for Kirby Churchyard.'

So he was. Over the brow of the hill before us could be seen a whitish patch streaming up in the direction of the old stone church. I clapped spurs to Boadicea, and had only just time to overhear the remark, 'That's Jack Ollyatt's mare . . . going like a top all day

. . . wasn't at the meet, though . . . by Jove, she 's worth all three hundred,' before it seemed we were toiling up the next valley.

All things considered, I fancy few were sorry for our first (and only) check.

It was about twenty past one by Kirby clock as a scanty dozen of us pounded up the deep muddy road, bounded on one side by the high wall skirting the garden of the Archdeacon, an eminent divine and *squarson*, albeit of somewhat fly-blown repute in the fox-hunting world. Along the other side was the churchyard, a long plateau of ground covering the crest of the hill, below which lay in parallel terraces the few streets of the homely little town of Kirby, where Cromwell lodged and fought, as more than one of its old stone walls and oak doors can still testify.

The scene it presented at that moment was such as could only be witnessed in the shires.

One pack or another ran by the place or through its outskirts once a week, very likely, throughout the season. Nevertheless, the twanging of a horn in the streets, the sound and the spectacle of scattered hounds careering about the churchyard, of dismounted huntsman and whip running this way and that in top boots, the hurried tramp of a score of horses' feet across the little market-place (where, by the way, there is a 'meet' every Christmas week, an assemblage vaguely suggestive of some local or Jacobite 'rising' of the 17th or 18th century, but better attended), brought all the inhabitants into the streets in five minutes. Rustics left their work. Maid-servants in caps and aprons ran out of the parsonage and the larger houses and villas to gain a point of vantage in the garden from which to view the excitement. The idler population crowded along the streets, and scattered across the fields and gardens and trim allotments that lay below the old town, wildly gesticulating and yelling. One already famous individual had seen the fox. 'He had actually crossed the churchyard, jumping (would it be believed of Reynard in a hurry?) over old Parson Wylie's grave!'—'He was in the vicarage garden.'—'He was in Farmer Ayston's spinney just below.'—'No; a labourer digging potatoes had seen him slink out at the far corner.'—'He had run up the ditch below the Cottage Hospital.'—'He had gone to ground in the big drain. Dan'l Ingram's terrier would have him out in no time.'

Forthwith the irregular chorus of the hounds hustling about in the little firwood beyond the parsonage (at the corner of which a groom was holding the whips' horses) was swelled by the baying and yapping of every mongrel in the place, and our small group of horsemen was soon surrounded by a crowd of aproned shop-men, loafers, and school-children, which seemed likely to obstruct further progress.

Being as impatient to get clear of this admiring mob as Louis XVI. to escape from the inhabitants of Varennes, I took the hint of a brown-gaitered bucolic, and trotted after him down a narrow lane, with a blank wall, half of the native rock, on one side, and commanding a view of numerous backyards and pigsties on the other. 'They'll work out below the Union,' he said; 'you follow me, master,' and I followed him. I have never been down that lane since, but 'in my mind's eye, Horatio,' I can see it now! We had not trotted a couple of hundred yards, and a few riders and a large part of the crowd seemed to be coming after us. The virtue of our short cut had not yet been disclosed, and meanwhile the town shut out, but for an occasional glimpse, all view of what might be going on in the fields below.

It was at this point that I heard a sound that sent a cold shudder down my back, nothing less than a lusty 'view-holloa' from within, as it seemed, fifty yards' distance. It was followed by a deafening outburst from the pack, the irregular baying, snarling, and shrieking of foxhounds that have found, are finding, or mean to find, a temporarily lost scent. The thought of hounds getting clear away while one pottered about cooped up in a little back street, was maddening. Our trot became a scurrying canter over rough ground, where the bed-rock (we were just below the old castle) shows up here and there in slippery patches. The crowd behind pressed after us cheering and jabbering.

Then there opened to the left a small lane with a gate at the end of it—'locked,' said one local authority, 'and it don't lead nowhere,' added another. As to that one could judge for one's self.

We could not only hear but, between the houses on each side, see the hounds. Three or four old stagers in line bellowing with muzzles deep in the grass, the rest scattered over the whole surface of a wide water-meadow, and screaming out impossible hopes and suggestions before subscribing to the wisdom of the aged. I trotted Boadicea carefully down that lane, and checked her with a view to exploiting a way out. She seemed to stumble; but it has often been said that there is no secret so close as that between a horse and his rider. Boadicea did not disclose hers till I was clinging helplessly about her ears in the middle of one of the small plots of garden into which the gate had led us, but no one else, amid the quenchless laughter of the enthusiastic citizens of Kirby. They were certainly well provided with allotments, though this was before the days of Councils; so I should have said from the number of small fences, we 'rocking-horsed' over in the next two minutes. At the second I hung round the neck of the beloved mare; at the third she threw me gracefully back into the saddle, and I recovered a stirrup or two, amid fainter cheers. Fortunately my light weight seemed to have no effect on her equilibrium; while, as to steering, she could see the hounds (a fact I might have realised sooner), and without being in any particular hurry, had no notion of spending the afternoon looking over a three-foot fence into a cabbage garden.

Soon clear of the outskirts of Kirby, and comfortably settled in the saddle, I pulled her into a gentle canter. In fact there was no hurry now. As we scrambled through a broken hedge in the fallow on the crest of that last hill, a belated puppy, squealing with new delight, disappeared through the opposite fence like a bolting rabbit.

And here it began to be apparent for the first time exactly what kind of run we were in for—no mere brilliant 'twenty' or 'thirty-five' minutes, no chronic run of this or that 'season,' but one transcending the two and a half hours of Billesden Coplow, and the finest traditions of Meynell or Tom Smith—a *day*, in fact, of red letter and white chalk, to be talked of in smoking-rooms, and over market dinners forty years after, and even celebrated afterwards in execrable verses by country gentlemen, whose seats were a good deal more certain than their scansion. For we had now worked up to the heights overlooking a new vast and open 'country'—a new world that lay unrolled before us like an old-fashioned map, with every field of its endless pastures, and every tree, it almost seemed, distinctly marked as far as eye could see (which is, in honest truth, over the borders of ten counties)—that 'vale,' famous in story, the first view of which is enough to convince any well-mounted lover of 'sport' that Eternal Providence in laying out this fair island had one great purpose in view, that men might ride hard and straight, and foxes die glorious deaths for the benefit of the lords of creation.

Of the few of us who that afternoon looked down that valley, none had much reason to regret our first and only check. Not that there was any stopping to admire the view. The pack, now drawing together, were forging ahead of us every minute, and it was impossible to lose them in a country where a single hound might almost (as they say of lights in the Channel) be 'visible at five miles in fine weather,' and only one large cover was within the horizon.

The string of customers among whom I found myself were, I fancy, mostly second horsemen, but of this we recked nothing, only that whenever we landed within ten yards of one of them, I could have told it blindfolded from Boadicea's wilful snatches at the bridle. The 'second wind' of a hunter—a phenomenon once much discussed by specialists—became to my young experience a positive and reassuring fact. It is also a fact that I was pulling her when, a couple of miles later on, she pounced with such admired deliberation in and out of the railed embankment of the great wood above West Felton. But, if I may quote the poem above mentioned (from an ancient number of the *Sporting Magazine*, in its faded blue cover)—

> ''Twere long to tell the steeds that fail
> As sweeps the chase through Wayland vale ;
> How fiercely mute the pack pursued,
> O'er field and fallow, rail and road ;
> What fagged ones saw with sad surprise
> These endless lines of fences rise ;
> What reins were tightened at the view,
> Of Wayland's current broad and blue.'

I doubt if there were eight of us ever reached this last obstacle, but whether there were six or ten, one and all felt, and sat and rode, as if the laurels of a fame, like that of the survivors of the Light Brigade, were already encircling his furry topper or draggled velvet cap.

It was ungrateful of me to regret that Boadicea jumped so far into the river (forty feet of water that no mortal steed ever yet cleared), but the vociferous and unintelligible directions of an Irish whip, who complained, while swimming with one hand on his saddle, that I should 'drown him intoirely' (there was no bridge near, and the pace was too good to look for a ford), seemed to excite her, and I had slipped the rein for a second. For, as it happened, we landed, with a crash like that of a hippopotamus at play, in a muddy shallow which saved me the complete ducking I expected.

Wet as a rat, of course, and at fever heat, I can't think she was ever really blown that day. At the last moment I showed my gratitude 'for all that we had received,' by asking, and not in vain, for a *leetle* more. It was all easy going, I said to myself, I only wanted in the intoxication of boyish vanity to be by the side of the master. There was no one in front of him, and then——

Not more than four or five lived through the delirium of that final ten or twelve minutes.

For the finish came all too soon on the far side of Dewberry Park. We must have come in by the corner just below the big pheasant cover—but one had lost all count of topography—as I remember that a purple bedraggled whip, with raised arm and half-shut eyes, came tearing down out of the ragged copse on my left, and gripping his jaded horse with hand and heel, flung through a rough bull-finch, expressing an intensely profane hope that it was the last.

It might have been had we killed in the park, for as we brushed over that fence I saw the hounds, a diminished stream, like one torn, waving, speckled hide, mute but for an occasional breathless shriek, scudding not fifty yards before us, and fast by some magic thread to the straining wisp of dark red that sped so arrow-like across the greensward.

* * * * *

'Does one want to kill the fox?' humane people sometimes ask. Well, it is a strange thing, but on such occasions one feels very much at one with the hounds, and there is no room for doubt as to what *they* want.

Personally, of that, my first experience, I can avow at this date that I believe I felt that I could have killed and eaten that particular fox.

Man is a venatory, but not a logical animal. Having undergone an unusual amount of acutely mixed sensations since first mounting Boadicea on that eventful morning, I had a vague feeling that the luckless, mischievous brute was somehow at the bottom of it all, and that his destruction would be a satisfying revenge for the now half-forgotten pangs of a compulsory education in 'straight riding,' compressed, as it had been, into a fiercer five minutes than I have ever known since.

The long row of old gables peeped higher and higher over the hill-side as the splendid chase—two miles of the most perfect turf in Great Britain, cut up by one or two dykes, at which no man or beast even looked—rolled out before us.

Fox and hounds, one streaming rag of colour, seemed to shoot away from us on the smoother slope.

It was but a last 'spurt'; and as the low railing and ha-ha, down which they vanished like water, drew near us, the master, with an anxious glance round at the rest of us, was already reining in.

Three of us abreast dropped over the fence on to a strip of roadway skirting the village green, pulled up haunch to haunch, and an elderly huntsman slid expeditiously from the saddle while the last scene of all was enacted under the nose of the snorting and steaming Boadicea. One last slip in landing had done for that gamest of quarries. A shriek, a flash of white teeth, a jangle of snarls, a tangle of red, black, and tan, and my first 'run,' except for those trophies presented by his lordship, and still venerated, was already a thing of the past.

* * * * *

The Squire of Dewberry, who, knowing the mare, kindly introduced himself to her rider, gave us of the good brown sherry and the oatmeal wash, both fully appreciated. A brief examination of the ordnance map, with mile-circles expanding from the large and verdant oblong representing his patriarchal domain, caused my youthful hair well nigh to stand on end. We were, it appeared, near thirty miles from home as the crow flies, and the faithful Boadicea, even when refreshed and rubbed down, could not imitate the flight of that intelligent bird. At doubtful points in the route I once or twice trusted to these 'instincts' of which one reads so much in works of fiction.

At that distance from her stable they failed to do more than involve us in a mile or so of extra walk ; an hour or so later in gathering darkness they served us better, and she broke into a home-going trot.

All excitement but a passion for repose had long vanished from her breast, but not from mine, as the familiar curve of woodland showed against the last yellow streaks in the cloudy sky, and the long row of lights winked in and out as we rounded the corners of the lime avenue. Arriving at what stay-at-home people loosely call 'the middle of the night,' the sound of heavy horse-hoofs on the gravel drive brought out a whole agonised household, and brought home to me the widely different emotions in which they and I had passed that eventful afternoon.

The glare of a couple of lanterns returning from one last fruitless search on the wrong highway had already illustrated the cardinal fact of our identity through the halo of mist from the steaming Boadicea. But great as was my delight to gratify these faithful searchers, what is the glare of a lantern to the glare of oaken logs ablaze on a good hall fire when the doors of home are flung wide to welcome a belated guest! Explanations—soon as I had dropped from the saddle and given a parting embrace to Boadicea—were, I fear, not even demanded.

Dinner, a late and anxious feast till interrupted by my arrival, seemed, after the necessary wash and change, an unusually bright and welcome reality, and perhaps the crowning satisfaction of the whole day was the brief apologue of our old family coachman who delayed the retiring procession of domestics after family prayers by stepping forward to observe laconically—

'The mare, Sir John, *is hall right.*'

* * * * *

The mare—she sleeps these twenty years back in the lower paddock (the bridle she carried that day hangs in the hall by his mask and brush); you can read her name on the little tombstone; but I never can without a sigh for the shortness of life allotted to certain friends of man, who carry so much of our affection to their early graves.

Well, well, there are other phenomena besides 'things of beauty' (not that Boadicea failed to answer that description) that never quite 'pass into nothingness.'

'You little *silly*,' said Alicia, the tall yellow-haired sister, with the petulance of despair; 'how often have I told you! You haven't the slightest *idea* how to fish properly. Oh, Philip, do come and look at Geoffrey. Just *fancy*, thinking he could catch a pike with a great *rope* like that!'

Master Geoffrey, a sturdy infant of eight and a half, upon whom this torrent of ironical reproaches fell like hail upon a sound roof, continued engrossed in the preparation of his fishing tackle for full half a minute before looking up with a smile on his fat rubicund cheeks.

'I'se tach one,' he said, in a tone partly apologetic, partly explanatory, 'of a *nunnerd year old!*'

'Fiddlesticks!' said Alicia, tossing her hair. She liked to get all the lines ready herself.

'You may catch one that's blind and deaf,' added the erect and scornful Philip, with silvery distinctness.

'*Oo-oof!*' retorted Master Geoffrey (the monosyllable was his usual expression of indignation). 'Fisses can't *hear!* oo-oof! you stoopid!'

Perhaps it was well they couldn't.

The deep bay-window of the large oak-panelled room in which the children played —and 'messed,' as nursemaids phrase it—directly overlooked a slaty-grey tract of water surrounding the old four-square 'fortified house.'

On the one side it seemed a dreary mere, on the other a sluggish stream some forty feet wide, the ancient moat which in days of looser orthography had given the place a name famous in story.

On its surface you might often see the pike lie basking of a sunny afternoon, one, two, three black streaks, each easily mistakable for a rotten stick.

Could any fish of discretion have looked in at the low open window he might have seen a terrifying sight—something which would have sent him darting off round the corner of the ivy-clad walls, and shaking up their rich reflected green with undulations like those of a painted stage-curtain, into the depths of the lake beyond—so awful and complicated was the apparatus which Master Geoffrey was putting together under such serious difficulties.

The only bit of eight-plait silk line with which they had ever entrusted him he had lost—

'Of course,' said Alicia and Philip together, 'and we shan't ever give you another bit.'

Their ingenious little brother had apparently foreseen this when he provided himself with a hank of some material rather stouter than blind-cord. To this he had, with a vague sense of proportion, attached a large salmon-hook, which, being devoid of plumage, he had some time since been allowed to add to the store of his infantine treasures. There remained only the question of bait.

'You can have that whopping great dace in the can, if you *like*,' said Alicia scornfully. 'It's much too big, of course, but it won't live till to-morrow anyhow.' And being supplicated with a little flattery she condescended to crown the absurdity of the whole process by fastening it on by means of two threads passed round the wretched creature's body, according to the precepts of Izaak Walton diluted through the illustrated *Angler's Guide* that lay open on the sofa.

'Let me frow it in,' said the expectant Geoffrey; but as Alicia and Philip agreed that if this were allowed there would be no chance of catching a pike even of one year old, the request was urged no further. The elder sister leant out of the bay-window and made a long arm, and the whole 'contraption,' as Philip called it, subsided into the water with a dull splash.

'Oh!' sharply exclaimed Alicia, at the same moment, 'if that ninny hasn't been and left another bare hook tied on to the line.'

The two elders were almost too scornful for words. 'A jolly fat lot,' said Alicia, 'you're likely to catch!'

Geoffrey quailed before her withering glance. 'I tieded it on,' he said modestly, 'and forgetted all about it.' He did not dare to avow the secret hope he cherished (had there been another bait left) of catching two monster fish; though what he would do with them when once firmly hooked, or they with one another, was a matter which he had not seriously considered. . . . The infant's idea of a centenarian pike was not entirely fanciful. He had heard his elders talk of a fish taken scarce a generation ago in this very water, and believed, on the curious evidence of a piece of antique tackle still hanging from its gills, to be at least more than half a century old. Dead and wasted, a bony monster with hideous lantern jaws—still to be seen in the county museum at Chapswich—it had scaled over forty pounds. Was it a unique specimen? No one could say. Some of the anglers privileged to experiment were confident they had seen, and some that they had even hooked and lost fish of larger size. In so large a tract of carefully-preserved and sequestered 'cover,' in the dark pool beneath the turret, in the dense bed of water-lilies that ran the whole length of the west side of the house, no one could say what might lie hid, beyond those things which no observant spectator or sportsman could fail to notice. On quite a recent occasion a gardener, struck by the persistence with which one of the swans (a full-grown bird of years of discretion) kept its head under water, had paddled out in the rude punt usually moored at the corner steps, and discovered the bird's head wedged tight into the mouth of another fine specimen of the *Esox Lucius*. Both were dead.

Then there was the pretty little toy-terrier belonging to a lady who called on the Reresby family one lovely summer afternoon. Having been left behind at the lodge, the excitable little animal essayed, on an imperious call from its mistress, who showed herself at the drawing-room window (all the living rooms look over the water), to cut off two corners by swimming.

In fact it had nearly done so, when, to the creeping horror of the few spectators, the pointed form of an ugly tarred gatepost was seen to float quickly up into the wake of that little dog. Not till they heard it shriek—not till the wretched little beast cried to its agonised and helpless mistress not four yards distant (like White of Selborne's beloved bunny, carried off shrieking under its owner's very eyes)—did anybody realise what had happened. Whatever the reader in his arm-chair may think, it was a grisly scene.

There was no splash to speak of, only a long

black shadow, a hollow swirl in the water, and a wave that broke stiffly against the wall just below the window-sill. After that no one seemed to have any appetite for tea, or admiration for the view, though the farther shore was ablaze with bright flowers; and the lady-caller drove home soon afterwards in bitter tears.

Beyond the fringed edge of the water-lily bank, whose broad overlapping leaves, seldom ruffled and flapped by any intruding wind, seemed to spread a smooth and solid carpet over the water, and whose long tangled stalks made a dark forest below, there was a tract of clear deep water. Nevertheless, many had said they would rather fish than bathe there, doubtless because the bottom was muddy. But the curious incidents above mentioned, and the seclusion and mysterious quiet, not to say gloom of the surroundings, enforced by certain local traditions, had somehow given the place an uncanny air. The last life-tenant of this ancient estate, a distant relative of the Sir Cuthbert Reresby who occupied it at the date of these events, passed the life of an eccentric anchorite, and the few who knew him report that the old man had strange habits and interests, that he spent long lonely hours on the old wooden seat let into the camp-shedding of the bank, feeding the fish and studying their habits, that he even purchased strange varieties and monstrous specimens, and that some died, and others became tame with a tameness rather alarming to the uninitiated.

They would eat live or dead fish dropped from your hand, and your hand itself, or any other part of you, if they got the chance. So some persons alleged, comparing the brutes to the lampreys of Vedius Pollio's villa which were fed, one reads, 'on the flesh of disobedient slaves.'

Years ago a school-boy—so ran one legend—overpowered by the novel interest of the situation, had clambered out of his bedroom window one breathless summer night, and sat in his night-dress, as boys will do, dangling his bare feet above or in the water. A few moments later sleepers on the first floor were wakened by a loud splash and a yell, sounds eternally associated with water in the minds of anxious parents. The boy, however, was found to have run back to bed, and woke the next morning in a raging fever.

He is said to have said—perhaps in a state of delirium—that some one threw a pavingstone at him!—a pavingstone which 'grazed his foot'! The fever might have been caused by the damp situation of the Mote—though the house, by the way, stood on gravel.

Moreover, being like most dwellings of its class, few of which have survived in so perfect a state, a hollow square with a courtyard and trim grass plot in the middle, it was a troublesome place to live in, or perhaps one should say, to live up to.

The perpetual labour of having to walk twice the necessary geographic distance, with the alternative of tripping across wet grass and a muddy drive, in order to get anywhere, was scarcely balanced by a crowd of historical associations, and the unusual excitement of being able to fish out of your bedroom window—though, of course, it was impossible from that position to land anything of greater weight than half a pound. On the delight afforded to children—for example, to the spoilt but entertaining nephews and nieces of Sir Cuthbert—by such a pastime it is needless to enlarge.

Geoffery Adalbert, before following the others

to tea in the nursery on the first floor, looked round for some secure object to which to belay the line of his complicated 'angle.' He had passed it round the table leg, when the brilliant idea occurred to him—why not make a mooring of the bell handle, and thus secure an early announcement of the arrival of the 'nunnerd-pound' pike? A smaller quarry would indeed scarcely have been able to make itself heard. To think—at least to think of anything original, and therefore probably illicit—is with such a child to act, unless restrained by interfering elders. In another minute Master Geoffrey, secretly exultant, vaguely apprehensive, and cautiously reticent, was upstairs grazing on a large sheet of bread and jam.

* * * * *

Reresby Mote, the reader may have inferred, was one of those strange old-world homesteads which make the romantic secrets of 'the provinces,' those regions whose diverse individuality seems so inexhaustible, that dreamland where the distance of a few leagues from the 'Sturm und Drang' of modern life seems often to equal that of as many centuries.

Curious tourists, visiting the well-known

manufacturing town of Helmingham, after driving out a dozen miles into the country, often experienced considerable difficulty in finding this relic of mediævalism to which they had been vaguely directed. They were usually told it was three, or four, or five miles farther on. At a later stage they sometimes inquired for Reresby Hall, and were shown—to their infinite disgust—a large brand-new red brick edifice erected by a retired merchant on a part of the once vast Reresby domains, which had since passed into other hands. For antiquarians indeed the correct name of the place was 'dog's-eared,' by a special knowledge of the mysterious and almost unknown distinction attaching to it—that, to wit, of a local *title*, ancient and now disused. Such persons would accordingly inquire at the little village of Reresby-Manton, for the road to the ancient family seat of the 'Lords Manton of Reresby Mote.' A two-mile drive from this, the nearest hamlet, over dreary and barren moor, and past long tracts of unkempt woodland, at last repaid the observer. From the crest of the nearest hillside you looked down over the intervening fringe of dark fir-wood on what seemed at first sight a rectangular island of grey stone in the middle of a vast and dreary lake. The mere, with its mysterious solitudes 'undisturbed,' said the county guide-book, 'since Anglo-Saxon times,' did, in truth, cover but two sides of the house, narrowing gradually to the width of what might otherwise have been itself regarded rather as a lagoon than a moat.

Not the least curious of its antique features was a genuine drawbridge which, it was said, had been up and down every night and morning for six hundred years. A melancholy but venerable butler would interpret the family motto *Aquâ et Armis*, and hint of the strange vicissitudes which the forbidding old mansion had passed through during the long years since those words were graven in the stone above the gateway, and point you, with scarce a quaver in his voice, to a damp and slimy stone staircase leading '*into* the moat, sir.' The dismal solitude of the house seemed to require a protection, the efficacy of which had been singularly illustrated by an uncanny modern incident. Being practically unapproachable at night, it was unprovided with the common defence of shutters, and even indifferent as to the closing of plate-glass windows and postern door.

But the nineteenth-century housebreaker, to whom nothing is sacred, and old silver the more attractive in proportion to its distance from a police-station, had essayed one frosty night to walk across the intervening strip of water at its narrowest point. By reason, however, of his ignorance of the ancestral family practice of breaking their ice at the edges (as others would bar their doors before retiring for rest), he had disappeared, and his body—pursued with one does not quite know what degree of enthusiasm—had never been seen again. For the rest, visitors, it will have been surmised, were few; and during the past generation had been unadmitted, if not unknown. Not for many a long year had the panelled walls and long oak passages resounded to the voices of children; and now again, after what has been that house's crowning experience in mysterious horrors, those voices are silent, and the house deserted.

* * * * *

The clanking of the old rusty chain on its wheel duly followed the last stroke of eight from the clock in the turret; and if it were true that the sound had re-echoed through the courtyard some hundred thousand times before, it might have seemed strange that any denizen of the place should on this particular evening appear surprised by it. But Mr. Jabez Benslee, B.A., who at the moment was stooping over the drawer of a mahogany writing-table in Sir Cuthbert's study, rose from that attitude with a guilty start.

For the tones, familiar enough in past years, suddenly proclaimed to him his present position as that of a thief and a burglar. Burglary, as Mr. Benslee knew, for he had acquired a smattering of law as an attorney's clerk before he first undertook the post of private secretary to the baronet, comprises not merely breaking into but breaking out of a house after entry with a certain *animus*, and an animus of some quasi-criminal kind glared out of the ex-private secretary's eyes as it flashed upon him that, by a ridiculous piece of negligence, he had allowed his retreat to be cut off.

He was a small, mean, insignificant man, whose commonplace vulgarity was overlaid by an uncongenial coating of education.

Sir Cuthbert's naturally charitable disposition

had made the most of this latter characteristic as an excuse for admitting Mr. Benslee—a poor and struggling relative—to a position of confidence in his household.

The connection had never been a very satisfactory one, and had a few days before terminated abruptly. The difference had arisen from an excessive taste exhibited by Mr. Benslee, who was really a very competent secretary, for the study of genealogy. Having for a year or more had the run of the house and library, with free access (freer than was ever intended) to the family papers, this ingenious gentleman, whose antiquarian enthusiasm was actualised by a keen regard to the main chance, had made an important discovery. It amounted to no less than the strongest possible evidence against the legitimacy of his employer's birth and consequent title, as a genuine Reresby, to the Mote estate.

This was obviously a serious matter, and the documents revealing it he had safely bestowed for the time—until the occasion should arise for its safe and effective employment—in a disused drawer, where the rightful owner would not be likely to find them. Further researches would, he hoped, establish his own title as a person possessed of valuable information to a reasonable but satisfying amount of hush-money, or blackmail. But events had been precipitated, chiefly, it may be said, owing to a particular species of list slipper worn by Sir Cuthbert on the evening in question.

Mr. Benslee's sense of hearing, as befitted a confidential employee, was tolerably acute. But, standing in close proximity to a private drawer recently opened by force or fraud, with the exasperated baronet's hand upon his collar, his first feeling was—that a gentleman should not wear list slippers. The irascible old gentleman was perhaps not guiltless of design in the matter.

He lived, indeed, remote from all worldly experience, shrinking from publicity, perhaps, as some men half-consciously do upon whose birth rests something of a cloud ; for though, as it happened, the rightful owner of the Mote property, he was no true Reresby, and in fact bore a title—this being the only act that lay on his conscience—which the law would have regarded as extinct.

Thus, or partly thus, it came about that his secluded home was but enlivened during part of the year by the presence of a young widowed sister, to whose children the reader has been introduced, or by occasional visits from bachelor friends of his own generation.

Sir Cuthbert passed the time not occupied with the duties of a landlord in the compilation of one of these harmless, if not very valuable, literary monographs which so often amuse the evening of a country gentleman's life.

Hence the private secretary.

The researches of the latter had gone so far that upon their discovery certain elementary confidences had become necessary. Upon their conclusion, when his employer found—as the climax of his suspicions of base ingratitude and low-prying curiosity—that he was confronted, as he phrased it, by a cold-blooded and scheming thief, temper got the better of prudence, and Mr. Benslee was actually and with threats and execrations kicked out of the house.

Stinging shame of the conscience-made cowardice with which the secretary had submitted to this, curdled all the conventional goodness in him to sour and sophistical malevolence. One of the two, he or his employer, must be a downright villain. The conclusion, if accomplished with a painful wrench of the moral system, was inevitable; and then the exposure of whatever could be exposed now became a positive duty, the past kindness of the injured party a gratuitous personal wrong.

Such was the 'animus' that sent Mr. Benslee back, on the evening of the events here related, desperate in his determination by one skilful manœuvre to secure the damaging document which he had bestowed as already mentioned, and then to exhibit himself, from a safe distance, as despot of an unpleasant situation.

The violence of that temper that rides a weak man like a scriptural devil made up for his lack of personal bravery. Hatred of the injured party who had revealed to him his own criminality filled him to the full with that malice aforethought which needs but the overt act to startle the world as—murder. He would not be defeated—spurned—again by that old dotard—his stifled anger added an epithet decrying his charitable old patron's birth. In fact, a slight social distinction or two—inevitable, had he the tact to see it—had been a constantly grating irritation. This flamed to natural fury after his 'counter-jumping' body had felt the superiority of that aristocratic old man's athletic training, as exhibited in the easy expulsion of his sneaking employé. Under all which circumstances it may be concluded that the hard implement concealed under the defiant Mr. Benslee's coat was something of a levelling nature calculated to assist him in his enterprise.

To return, indeed, after taking up his quarters at the little hostel in the distant village, to wait concealed in the near belt of woodland for a quiet occasion, and then slink in the dusk across the drawbridge and round the courtyard to the spot where he now stood, was a matter of little serious difficulty. The walk had perhaps been longer than he calculated, and the lateness of the hour had somehow momentarily escaped him. He would have sworn that it was the half-hour and not the three-quarters that he had last heard clang from the turret. Even now that two quick strokes of the bell had gone there would possibly have been time for an active young man to have scuttled across the stone-paved square and, braving the chance of arrest, made his way out before the clumsy and ancient causeway had left the farther bank. But the private secretary lacked nerve, and the reverberation of the sing-song notes, re-echoing from the surrounding walls, seemed to fill the courtyard with a sort of publicity, which he shrank from facing, like that of a crowd of people.

While he hesitated, the clanking bridge swung up and darkened the archway, shutting out the last fading rays from the cloudy autumn sky.

Mr. Benslee, with his hand still upon the study-door, stood looking through the passage window into the vacant courtyard. The object of his visit having been secured, the question of escape—serious, but as yet scarcely terrifying—engrossed his faculties. A soft misty rain had been falling for an hour or so. In the west wing, almost at the farthest corner of the mansion, he could see through the red blinds the blurred lights in the council-room (not the dining-hall, which was only used on state occasions), where the family, a party of not more than three or four, were, as he well knew, at their early dinner. But for his own owlish and abandoned stupidity—so did this unrepentant thief execrate himself—he might have been a respectable sharer in that repast. He stepped softly towards the end of the passage—his tennis-shoed feet clinging close to the creaky oak flooring. The men-servants, he reflected, would be occupied for an hour to come; but a housemaid, if she were not already tidying the long drawing-room, might pass and observe him. In any case a hiding-place, desirable at the instant, would in a short while be essential.

Just before him opened a large dark panelled room with a bow-window formed by the north-eastern turret of the Mote, a room carelessly furnished and in apparent disorder. The ex-secretary, who knew its appearance well, remembered that it contained one or two large and deep cupboards which he thought were seldom opened. There were others farther down the corridor itself.

At such a moment, halting in poignant anxiety and a half-light, imprisoned in the familiar but now hostile ancient house, it was perhaps not unnatural that he should think of 'the ghost.' There are one or two tolerably well-authenticated examples of the supernatural in almost every English county, but the Reresby ghost differed from these not merely in the unfamiliar rarity of its visits—which might have left it a mere legend—but in their epoch-making nature, when they did occur.

The Royalist captain in armour, whose proper place was (or, at least, whose external habiliments hung) in the old hall to which you enter to the right of the porch, could scarcely be said to 'haunt' the Mote. But on certain indeterminate occasions, once or twice in a century, he solemnly 'went the rounds,' as of yore in life, when an inadequate Roundhead force had battered with their culverins the patches still visible in the eastern wall. The occasions of his visits—rare enough by the testimony of mortal eyes—seemed, unless this were preposterous coincidence, not ill-chosen. Once, it was told, a fraudulent steward in the act of absconding with ill-gotten gains had been arrested (the story is locally well known) and terrified into confession by the appearance—real or fancied—of this grim warrior, and the gleam of the moonlight upon his breastplate and portentous halberd. At a later date, not a hundred years ago, a would-be murderer of a higher class—the variants of the grisly tradition cannot here be rehearsed—had been found in a dying condition at this very spot, where the floor still showed, in strong sunlight, what might be the stains of blood. He had only, so ran one legend, had time to whisper the words 'I have seen him.' Others told that at least one surviving witness had at the same moment seen and heard a figure, *in armour that rattled*, disappear under the carved archway at the far end.

These, however, were but trivialities to the fact certified on oath by the military surgeon and the priest. The latter had been called in, too late, to the help of a profligate and desperate scion of the house, against whose revengeful villainy that house had in such a mysterious fashion protected itself. There was no public inquest or inquiry; but the surgeon, who knew nothing either of the identity of the criminal or of the family tradition, was professionally nonplussed by the nature of a wound inflicted, he averred, by no implement known to his science. The old Sir Philip, Lord Manton, had subsequently, and with very mixed feelings, conducted the fellow (whose curiosity it was advisable to satisfy as far as possible) through the armoury, and thence, in a stupor of suspense, into the entrance-hall above mentioned. There hung a dozen suits of armour, and, above one in particular, a hideous weapon, headed like some fanciful variety of ploughshare. 'Holy Boney!' said the surgeon, 'it was something just like that'; and he mounted a chair to examine the weapon.

'It's been there a hundred and fifty years,' stammered the old baron. 'It's fastened to the wall, man.'

So it was, with heavy nails and thick, rusted iron wire. The dust lay thickly upon the long shaft of the halberd, but there was something on the point that sent the surgeon quaking to the floor, whiter than he had ever been at his first operation. Then, so runs the exact tradition, they told him the story. His secrecy was secured by a handsome fee; and though it would be idle to say that his suspicions were allayed, they were believed to have been diverted from the world of flesh and blood.

A faint flavour of these legends, and their possible bearing on his own position, coloured the anxious imagination of Mr. Benslee, as a passing scent recalls to us a distant country scene. A vague fear of being seen in the dark passage by something which he could not see was just what caused him at that instant to beat a retreat from the ghost's corridor. Cautiously stepping inside the panelled room, he turned the handles of two large cupboards, each capable of holding two or three men, in succession, and noted that both contained a good many of those miscellaneous articles, familiar yet undefinable in the darkness, which usually accumulate in a country house. Under the circumstances this simple fact was maddening, for it was difficult to feel sure that such a retreat might not be invaded.

He moved down the room towards the large window, whose semi-circular arc gave a copious view, by daytime, in two directions.

To the right, close below the house which shut out from it all the waning light left in the western sky, lay the moat, black as ink and smooth as polished ebony, save where a scarcely distinguishable fringe of water-lily leaves lay like some curious carving that overlaps a dark framed print. To the left it broadened out into the mere, over whose grey surface, faintly streaked with silver, a soft fleecy mist was beginning to creep, obscuring with its white folds the dusky outlines of the distance. From round the angle of the building the silence was now and again broken by a deep sound as of water poured from a large bottle, echoed by fainter splashes from beyond the rolls of mist.

Out there, reflected the only spectator of the mysterious scene, there was secrecy and safety enough—if only——

What was he dreaming of? Why, at the steps in front of the southern wing lay the old punt, a crazy and leaky vessel, in truth, but at such a crisis more precious than the richest argosy to the boldest buccaneer. Immediately under the windows ran a narrow ledge of stone (supplemented here and there by a strip of muddy bank) on which it was surely possible to climb or creep in silence round to the library steps before the family dinner (carried on, it was to be remembered, in the next room) would be over.

With this somewhat desperate project Mr. Benslee opened the last window on his right hand. One on the left stood open, but he wished to save himself the circuit of the turret. Then with a second thought he drew back into the room and sat down on a chair to take his shoes off. The rubber, he said to himself, would slip on the wet stone; and if he had to swim for it, why——*What was that?*

A rustling sound as of a rat or mouse running over the wainscot of the farther wall checked at once the current of his thoughts and of his blood with apoplectic suddenness. Was it possible that the large and dusky room held some-one besides himself—a child?—a dog? Hastily tearing off and pocketing the other shoe, he rose, and stepped, listening intently, in the direction from which the sound had seemed to come. A dead silence followed, save that through the open windows came a dull deep plash, as of an oar lightly turned in the water. Mr. Benslee looked out in alarm. Could some one be moving the punt? No; it was his nervous fancy—everything was quiet. Then again after a second's pause came the same rat-like twitching, scraping rustle, but quicker and louder, till it was drowned by a more ominously unintelligible noise. He started back, stumbling against the chair, and execrating—to himself—a rent in the carpet. And then, just after (or just before?) his movement, something *snapped* like a trap shutting in the middle of the wall; and a third time, to his fevered imagination, it seemed that some small light animal trailed or scurried by him, this time in the direction of the bow-window, and there vanished.

There was no time to think what it was, for on the instant a furious peal from a bell somewhere in the offices resounded through the house. Long before its reverberations had ceased, the door at the north end of the passage was flung briskly open, and a maidservant, after pausing for a moment at the door of the room in which Mr. Benslee stood, fled down the corridor, with loud exclamations of surprise and alarm.

In a moment the house seemed to be alive with 'feet that ran and doors that clapped,' and it became apparent to the ex-secretary that his presence was no longer a secret, and would shortly be the object of general attention. With longing eyes did he gaze at the dusky belt of firwood that covered the slope on the opposite bank of the moat. The water was too deep, even if the bottom were sound, for wading: but the distance after all was nothing to the most ordinary swimmer. Consequently, as the sound of heavily-booted feet was now audible coming down the corridor, Mr. Benslee with reluctant expedition scrambled over the window-sill and slid down into the dark oily water.

He had not swum half a dozen yards before lights flashed into the room he had just left, and their reflections danced about the disturbed surface of the moat. He could hear the buzz of excited voices from the house behind him, and though spurred to frenzy by the mere fancied contact of a single trailing lily-stalk—there was usually a clear passage at this point—he spread his arms for another stroke as quietly as possible. But at that moment an agonising stab of pain, so acute that it seemed to penetrate the whole body at once, arrested his course and seemed—by what paralysis or compulsion he could not tell—to be dragging him under the water.

* * * * *

Sir Cuthbert and his half-brother, the Colonel, surrounded by a medley of chattering servants and two ladies in a state of almost hysterical alarm, stood in the turret-room, hastily examining the walls, the cupboards, the furniture, by the light of guttering hand-candles, which, however, revealed nothing unfamiliar.

'Letty, be sensible,' said the baronet, grasping his second housemaid by the elbow. ‘You say you 're absolutely certain—Edith, darling, there 's nothing in the world to be alarmed about—that this was the bell that rang. Ronald, just take the light a minute, I don't see——’

‘Pardon me, sir’—it was the valet, a spare, quiet young man in black, who pushed forward to speak—‘that handle's been pulled out of place—a sharp blow, sir. Something must 'ave fell on it.’ On a closer scrutiny this seemed a probable enough suggestion, but that there was neither anything to fall nor anything which appeared to have fallen.

‘You say you saw a man—Edith, dear, go up and see after the children; they may be frightened—standing in the middle of the room?’

‘That 's what she said, sir,’ chimed in butler and footman, dissatisfied with their secondary share in the sensation.

‘Then—I wish you wouldn't all talk at once—he must have got out—Parkins, take all those girls to the servants' hall—by the window—and bring a bull's-eye lantern.’

The two men advanced to the bay of the turret and looked out, Sir Cuthbert holding a light over the water. In the still air the candle burned steadily, but its feeble flame served but to make the darkness of the water and the surroundings more impressive.

In a moment, however, the figure of a man, swimming with difficulty, was indistinctly visible.

'I see,' said the master of the house, the hostile instinct of the chase waking within him, 'he is trying to get across that way. Roberts, run for the punt and head him off.'

The able-bodied young footman had already scampered down the passage, and was soon heard frantically paddling the leaky oblong vessel round the corner of the house. Meanwhile the three other men, in strangely excited suspense, waited and watched the escaping quarry. It was obvious, though distances could not be exactly discerned, that the punt would not intercept him.

'Have the drawbridge down and I'll run round,' said the Colonel, 'and take 'em in the rear.'

But further speculation was stayed and the suspense of the watchers and the pursuer brought to a head of overpowering horror by a shriek from without. It was a shriek long, almost articulate, but that something stifled its close, while what seemed the ghosts of words were still re-echoing along the walls of the Mote.

Sir Cuthbert Reresby staggered back blanched and trembling. The old butler, stumbling into the room, shook at him a large glowing lantern. The Colonel set his teeth and grasped the handles, turning the light steadily over the water. For a few seconds, no more—and that indeed was too long—it lit up the white staring face of a man standing, or striving to stand, breast-deep in the muddy shallows at about twenty-five yards from them. It is certain that the shriek from the figure's wide-opened mouth took the form of an articulated word, and the word, confounded by the reverberating echo from the walls, may possibly have been, as some averred, a cry for 'mercy'—the instinctive appeal of a human animal believing itself in weird and ghastly fashion trapped by indignant enemies, and crazed with the fear of something worse than death.

What it meant,—to whom the word could under the circumstances be reasonably addressed, no one could divine. Nor was colloquy possible. In a second the figure, just as Sir Cuthbert had identified it, was seen to stumble, subside, and reappear swimming in a strangely disordered fashion on the surface.

With the gathering night, and this sudden cropping up of the hideously unintelligible, the whole scene passed, dragging the reluctant *dramatis personæ* with it, from the sphere of a domestic or police tragedy into the region of raving nightmare.

The Colonel was a man not unfamiliar with danger and death, yet, after forcing the lantern into Sir Cuthbert's limp grasp, he flung out of the room, and across the courtyard, feeling the absolute necessity of action, however useless.

Perhaps only a Greek poet could have done justice to the scene—a *tableau vivant* of half-supernatural horrors clustering inevitably about a mere chain of acts and accidents only to be unified under the title of—*Fate*.

But a few seconds before, Sir Cuthbert had been an indignant landlord engrossed in the pursuit of a probable thief or housebreaker—a figure swimming across his moat, and possibly carrying away some of his property.

The figure was now moving or floating uneasily towards him ; but instead of deriving any satisfaction from this phenomenon he would have run away shrieking, but that his tongue seemed glued to his mouth and his feet to the floor—

For Mr. Benslee was swimming in the opposite direction! and the movements of the distraught figure, its jerks and dives—for once or twice it disappeared under the water—had the ghastly uncanniness—in a live or half-live creature—of a marionette moved by wires. For every yard it advanced towards him through the dark, lit by the shaking lantern still grasped convulsively in his hand, as if it were a weapon of defence, a fresh rain of perspiration poured down the old baronet's face.

The plash of the nearing punt came like rescue to the besieged. The athletic footman and his paddle must, it seems, meet and derange this awful object momentarily converging on to the same point in front of the window. And he or some one else would, of course, jump in and rescue the body—or the corpse. So it seemed. But precisely then, before any one could speak or think, supervened a crisis of horror which, till the very curtain fell on this incomprehensible tragedy, crushed out all power of thought from the spectators.

Immediately before them the water swirled audibly as from a mill-wheel, and from the dark trench made in it suddenly rose a *thing*, vast, black but for two gleaming rows of long white tusks, slimy to the light, and flapping plaques of water to right and left, and then descended in a mist of spray. One said it was a mad pig, another that it was headed like a hay-rake, but as to what it did all agreed.

The formless monster shot up with a noisy 'warp' out of the moat, stopped suddenly in the air, and fell with a crash. Before that, Mr. Benslee's ghost—or whatever it was—attempted, with a hideous appearance of frivolity, to kick the flying thing whilst it was in the air, a feat involving the submersion of the human head. Failing in this, the ex-private secretary disappeared again, perhaps from fear, obviously with a frantic effort, when the black pig-like thing, tusks and all, subsided almost upon him. And it crazed the helpless beholders to see, as the monster made off, leading a long V-like hillock along the surface, and occasionally showing a black fin or flapper above the water, towards the lake, that Mr. Benslee, still swimming in the peculiar fashion he seemed to have invented, followed its course.

The footman did not pursue the procession. He did not stay to look at it; but had clambered in at the window leaving the leaky punt unsecured, and now sat in the deepest of arm-chairs, his white face buried in his hands as if to shut out all further spectacles.

For the first instant the Colonel, who had returned to the room, and Sir Cuthbert, who had come back to himself, turned their eyes upon one another. Neither of them had anything to say—nothing perhaps even to express but the mute hope that the succession of phenomena, known as 'Time,' would not select this particular moment for any considerable halt. 'Nature' might then have a chance of reasserting herself.

* * * * *

When they looked again over the water there was nothing to be clearly seen, even with the lantern. Mr. Benslee had swum under the water-lily leaves. Mr. Benslee had concealed himself in the lake.

Under the circumstances, further pursuit seemed useless and unnecessary, though the water continued heavily to heave and roll as if something were still stirring somewhere. Overhead could be heard the wailing 'whoops' of a lusty-lunged child in strong hysterics. Night had enveloped the Mote.

* * * * *

But with the gradual re-awakening from nightmare to the more ordinary fever of mundane excitement and alarm the necessities of law and civilisation reappeared.

In the course of a few hours messengers had brought police, labourers from the village. Some one, it was told them, had fallen into the water and, it was feared, had been drowned. Thus instructed they brought a boat borne upon a cart, and even an elementary grappling-iron, with which a party of strangers explored for the first time the moat and lake. But though the lake was, as has been said, vast, the moat wide, the weeds many, the water deep and the mud deeper, it was matter of surprise to many of the searchers that no body was found.

Sir Cuthbert, in fact, made the only discovery, that of a small piece of paper soaked with wet, and lying on a water-lily leaf half-hidden by another. This he hastily thrust unobserved into his pocket.

But although the ex-private secretary escaped detection, it is not quite certain that he was never seen again.

For as the grey of dawn was beginning to spread over the lake, Sir Cuthbert sat in the Colonel's bedroom on the first floor in the north corridor. Neither had thought of trying to sleep, until at this moment drowsiness had invaded the former, whose pipe, most faithful of consolers, fell to the floor and broke. Sir Cuthbert swore nervously, which woke the dozing Colonel, who cast a glance out of the window before retiring to his own room.

In a second the awakened eyes of both were riveted on a persistent disturbance going on at the distance of about two hundred yards from the walls of the Mote.

Have you seen a score or so of coarse fish—roach or bleak—fighting for a floating crust of bread? or a dozen eels and perch struggling in close proximity on a tangled night-line? Mix and multiply, and you have the scene, indistinctly visible, in the dull grey dawn.

'What's the water there?' stuttered the Colonel.

The baronet's face was like a sheet. 'Shallows,' he murmured. Indeed a small dark streak in the middle might have been mistaken for a patch of mud but that it seemed to move now and then. About it the speckled water seethed and stirred. Then there was a splash audible to the lookers-on, and a large body rose and fell. Then the patch disappeared into the deeps, and there was silence.

* * * * *

It was a year later that two middle-aged ladies—Mrs. Gravelegh Hall and her sister—rented the Mote. The former in her capacity of artist had been vastly attracted by a description that promised interesting studies of reflections, 'moated-grange' effects—she was then engaged on her celebrated picture—and mediæval architecture.

All these she found, and more than could well be put into an estate-agent's catalogue. But being a strong-minded woman she stayed on ; nevertheless the gloom of the place was such that it was found necessary to muster a few cheerful friends, a 'forlorn hope,' though they knew it not.

Thus it came about that on one evening in autumn, five persons—the two sisters, a cousin from Ireland, and Mr. and Mrs. Albert Sinclair—sat in the room overlooking the water, the room that had been Sir Cuthbert's study.

'I have had these two comfortably refurnished,' said the hostess, with perhaps a slight accent of defiance. It was almost dark, and a servant had just brought in after-dinner tea, an institution in the household.

In the mere fact that a bell at that particular instant pealed sharply there would be nothing curious, if it had not been that the bell belonged to the next room, which was presumably unoccupied at the moment. The servant reappeared, looking slightly uneasy.

'Some more hot water,' said her mistress, rather as if she had just learnt the phrase by heart ; and then, pursing up her lips, sat down resolutely at the tea-table, like a patient at the dentist's awaiting an inevitable period of suffering.

Mrs. Sinclair, a young and pretty woman,

rose and walked to the window, which was slightly open, and leant out, excitedly calling from that position to her husband — 'Bertie, come here and look. There *must* be a big fish feeding out there.'

By that time every one in the room had heard *it*.

From the far side of the dusky water came the sound of a thick struggling splash, and the broken surface caught for an instant a gleam of the fading light.

'Good gracious! I wish it was lighter and one could see. Why, that must have been——'

A husky voice sounded a single eerie dissyllable into the room. It might easily have been another female note of admiration, a sequel to the 'good gracious!'—so the lady at the tea-table said to herself, regretting for the moment, not that it was difficult to see, but that it was not impossible to hear.

But the wife turned sharply to her husband. 'Did you speak, Bertie? No? . . . I thought some one said——'

'Do you take sugar?' interjected Mrs. Hall, whispering to herself 'the third time.'

'A man calling on the road beyond the fir-trees.'

'Is there an echo?'

'Come and have tea,' said the hostess firmly, 'or it will be black. Perhaps you'd shut that window. It gets rather chilly. Yes, and draw the curtain. Alice, will you play something,—*something loud*,' she added hurriedly aside to her sister. The latter, as the others sat down, moved towards the grand piano with an uncertain step, and before reaching it subsided limply into a chair, with her hands to her ears.

Then the sound of a heavy footfall in the passage was drowned by the horrid and ominous crash of a smooth bulky body falling heavily on the water.

Two women and the man sprang to their feet at once in alarm; one crying—

'Some one fallen in, Bertie; run and help.'

Mrs. Hall called faintly from her chair—

'It's no use, Mr. Sinclair, and—and—you'd better not open the door. We sometimes——'

But Mr. Sinclair was already in the corridor. In a moment the door slammed and he was back again in the room (like a hurried traveller who has forgotten something of vital importance) and stood by the tea-table, the others watching him statue-like in a stupor of surprise. Mrs. Hall touched his arm lightly.

'There was some one there?' she said steadily, as if to reassure the young wife and her other guest. Mr. Sinclair pulled himself together.

'Yes,' he answered, pouring a jug of milk into the tea-urn—'there was some one there.'

THE END

www.ingramcontent.com/pod-product-compliance
Lightning Source LLC
Chambersburg PA
CBHW021059030726
47496CB00006B/1915
9783337230715